Her cranky, surly nephew sat on the bare floor while a mother cat licked milk from his fingertips.

Nestled around the black-and-white cat was a bunch of brand-new baby kittens.

Derrick raised a rapt face. "She had babies. I watched."

Gena went to her haunches. "How many?"

"Four. She's really tired now." He sounded vulnerable and sweet, like the loving little boy he'd once been.

"I expect so." She stroked a finger across the mother cat's head. The animal seemed friendly. The big surprise to her was that Quinn Buchanon would own a cat. An attack-trained rottweiler, yes. But a cat?

She looked up at the bewildering man standing inside the door. Had she misjudged him?

He was watching her. Not Derrick or the cats but her. For ten seconds their eyes held. Gena suffered a dozen conflicting emotions—including completely unwanted attraction and a need to know the man behind the haggard face and bent, scarred arm.

Linda Goodnight, a *New York Times* bestselling author and winner of a RITA® Award in inspirational fiction, has appeared on the Christian bestseller list. Her novels have been translated into more than a dozen languages. Active in orphan ministry, Linda enjoys writing fiction that carries a message of hope in a sometimes dark world. She and her husband live in Oklahoma. Visit her website, lindagoodnight.com, for more information.

Books by Linda Goodnight

Love Inspired

The Buchanons

Cowboy Under the Mistletoe
The Christmas Family
Lone Star Dad

Whisper Falls

Rancher's Refuge
Baby in His Arms
Sugarplum Homecoming
The Lawman's Honor

Redemption River

Finding Her Way Home
The Wedding Garden
A Place to Belong
The Christmas Child
The Last Bridge Home

Visit the Author Profile page at Harlequin.com for more titles.

Lone Star Dad

New York Times Bestselling Author

Linda Goodnight

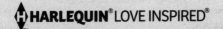

Recycling programs for this product may not exist in your area.

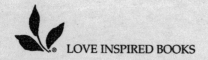

LOVE INSPIRED BOOKS

ISBN-13: 978-0-373-71982-2

Lone Star Dad

www.Harlequin.com

Printed in U.S.A.

Let us come boldly unto the throne of grace,
that we may obtain mercy,
and find grace to help in time of need.
—*Hebrews* 4:16

For family, who sustains me, and as always,
for the glory of Jesus.

Chapter One

He wouldn't do this. Not again. He wouldn't shame himself or his family this way.

Quinn Buchanon clenched his jaw hard enough to make his face ache and slapped his outstretched hands against the fireplace mantel. He was off balance, as always, the fingers of his right hand barely reaching, while the left was just dandy. The bitter root of the last eleven years curled inside his chest. His arm throbbed harder.

He glanced up at the plastic clock tacked above the crackling fireplace. Two o'clock. Too early.

Releasing a slow, frustrated breath, he pushed back and rubbed his right arm, the exact spot where the surgical titanium rod pushed against the bent muscle and scar tissue. On winter nights, the ache was worse. Add precipitation, like tonight's cold misty rain, and he was in a world of hurt.

Quinn had thought he'd conquered the problem during his stint in Dallas, but the last surgery and coming home to Gabriel's Crossing brought the pain and grief and most of all the pure exuberant thrill tumbling back in. The glory days. The accident. Yes, accident, as he'd come to realize last year. Jake Hamilton had not intended to hurt him. If anything, the fault was Quinn's. His own fault. His own misery.

Whoever was to blame, the damage was done and he'd never be the same. Most days, he didn't even feel like a man, certainly not the toast of Gabriel's Crossing and half of Texas that he'd once been.

Memories were killer.

Head starting to pound in that incessant ache he knew too well, he took long strides down the length of the cabin, through the living space and out onto the saggy front porch. The air would clear his head. The cold would give him something else to think about.

He liked the quiet, lonely spot here in the woods by the Red River where none of his well-meaning siblings—six of them—could casually drop by. He loved his family but he needed space.

A sharp, wet wind blew up from the river. Quinn reached back inside, grabbed his coat from the hook hanging next to the door and shrugged it on. He shoved his hands into his pockets but left his head bare. He lifted his face to the blast of wet air, needing the slap of cold.

The weathered old hunting cabin he called home was nothing fancy, but the rustic unpainted logs and bare-bones essentials nestled among the oak and cedar of northeast Texas suited him. The porch wasn't much, either, a wooden floor and a sagging overhang with a weathered rocking chair, a pile of firewood and a dead potted plant from his landscaper mother that he'd forgotten to bring in before the frost.

He sucked in the cedar scent, held the frigid air in his lungs until they ached and then let it out in one gusty breath.

The pawpaw tree two steps off the porch clung to a single leaf like a mother holds on to a child's hand in a hurricane.

He watched that one valiant leaf battle for life. When

at last the wind proved too much and the quivering leaf sailed into the mist, lost forever, Quinn felt a little sad.

Battling. Buffeted. Lost. He could relate. He was hanging on for dear life and didn't intend to let go, no matter how hard the wind slammed him.

A fine mist peppered his skin, soft rain edging toward sleet.

By tomorrow a thin sheen of ice would cover the grass and trees and sparkle in the sunrise. He'd be up. He always was. Sleep was short.

He settled in the rocker, a remnant from long-forgotten former owners, and tried to focus on the weather, the outdoors, the surrounding woods and creeks he'd loved since boyhood. Sometimes they helped. Sometimes not. Regardless, he wouldn't let himself go back inside the cabin for a while. Personal discipline was the one lesson he'd never quite learned off the football field, but he had to learn now.

He had work to complete for Buchanon Built Construction, his family's construction company. Maybe he could get his mind on a new set of architectural plans and off the pain.

He rubbed at his shoulder again, over and over. Up and down. Round and round. The ache went clear through his chest into his heart. Deeper yet, into his soul.

God seemed far, far away.

On the lane leading from the dirt road, the only road that connected him with anywhere, a shadowy creature appeared out of the mist. Quinn squinted through the drizzle. Maybe a raccoon. They were plentiful here. As the animal waddled closer, Quinn recognized a cat—a very pregnant cat, her belly swinging like a metronome.

He didn't much like cats.

Yet she was a distraction and he watched her trot in his direction until she reached the porch, stopped at the edge, raised her thin face and mewed. Her troubled eyes gleamed golden yellow in a black-and-white face.

Quinn looked away. "Sorry, lady. You're on your own."

She wobbled onto the porch and rubbed against his leg. He felt the bumpy movement of her unborn kittens and, startled, moved his leg.

"Go on, now. Get out."

She mewed again, gazed around the mostly empty porch. Finding no comfy spot, she sprawled across his feet.

Quinn gently slid his boot from under her disconcerting belly and went inside the cabin.

He hadn't intended to go inside. Temptation waited there, calling his name with promises of relief that ensnared. The cat had left him little choice.

As if she carried a megaphone, the pregnant feline meowed loud enough for him to hear through the solid wooden door. Quinn turned on the television and though he could no longer hear her, he knew she was there. He peaked out the window. She was in his chair, though how she'd gotten her swollen body up that high defied the laws of physics.

He couldn't leave her out there in the cold. What if she had those kittens? What if he awoke tomorrow morning to a pile of frozen baby cats on his front porch?

With a defeated sigh, he rummaged around until he found a cardboard box, dumped out the contents, added a couple of old towels and went back outside.

"You're not coming in the cabin. Understand? There's the well house. It's heated. Pipes freeze, you know." He motioned toward the leaning, unpainted building beside the cabin that housed the well and was where he kept his tools and basic man junk. "You can bunk there until this weather passes. No babies, though. You hear me? Tomorrow at the latest, you're out of here."

Gently, his stomach a little woozy when the kittens did

all kinds of gyrations against his hand, Quinn lifted her into the box. As if she'd been expecting exactly this, she settled into the towels. He toted her, box and all, to the shed and put her inside.

She blinked up at him with big golden eyes.

Quinn growled deep in his throat, muttered, "Sucker," and went back into the cabin for a bowl of warm milk.

He left the old girl lapping with her dainty tongue and jogged toward the porch. The mist spattered his face like tiny, cold pebbles.

From out of nowhere, a gunshot cracked the gray stillness.

Quinn whirled toward the sound. Blood roared in his ears. His heart thudded madly. It took all his willpower not to fall to the ground and low-crawl back to the cabin. He didn't, a small victory.

A gunshot in the woods echoed far and wide and was hard to pinpoint, but this one was close. Too close. Even though Buchanon land was posted, poachers invariably tried their luck this time of year.

He clamped his jaw tight and stomped toward his truck. This poacher's luck had just run out.

Someone was coming.

Gena Satterfield hung a tea bag on the side of a Nurse Practitioner Needs Chocolate mug, turned off the steaming kettle and walked through the house, curious. No one drove up that ungraded, potholed driveway, at least not without prior warning. The house was remote, exactly what she'd needed to keep Derrick out of trouble when they'd moved here last year.

At the front room window she tugged back the curtain and saw a black pickup bounce up the road. Someone would be mighty unhappy at the damage this driveway could do to a fancy truck like that. Whoever he might be, he was going too fast.

Gena watched, waiting to identify the driver. She didn't open her door to strangers.

The truck jolted to a halt. A man hopped out and slammed the door with a force that echoed through the woods.

Gena's breath froze in her chest. Quinn Buchanon.

What was *he* doing in her front yard? The one person in Gabriel's Crossing she preferred *never* to encounter one-on-one. Especially not in her own home.

Mouth suddenly dry as cottonseed hull, she stayed huddled behind the curtain. He could knock but she wouldn't open. Not to him.

He marched around the front of his truck, clearly in a fit of temper, yanked open the passenger-side door and hauled someone out by the scruff of the neck—a lanky eleven-year-old boy with a bad attitude.

"Oh, no. No, no, no!" Gena jerked at the knob, flinging the door wide to race down the steps in her fuzzy slippers, heedless of the gray, damp cold.

"Derrick! What are you—" She skidded to a stop, attention frozen on the rifle in the boy's hand. In a terrible voice, she asked, "Where did you get that gun?"

"I—"

Before he could respond, she whirled on the detestable man. This was exactly the kind of irresponsible thing someone like Quinn would do.

She jabbed a finger at him. "Did you give him that gun? Have you lost your mind?"

Quinn glared at her. "I was going to say the same to you."

"Me? I don't own a gun." She turned on the boy. "Where did you get that?" she asked again.

Derrick, mouth insolent, posture slumped, only shrugged. She hated when he did that, which was all too often.

"Tell me where you got that gun or no computer for a month."

He twitched. "Service out here sucks anyway."

"The deal still holds. Talk."

"I found it."

"*Found* a rifle? Where?" *Oh, Lord. Please don't let this be stolen.* She'd never dreamed raising a boy alone could be this hard.

"The storage room. I went hunting. It's no big deal. That's what *country* boys do, isn't it?"

His cocky, derisive attitude set her teeth on edge. He hated it here, deep in the country, away from the city, away from his so-called friends, away from taking things that didn't belong to him, but until today he'd been in less trouble in Gabriel's Crossing than in Houston. Less. He wasn't Boy Scout material yet. She kept praying for him to settle in and be the happy boy he'd once been.

Quinn, who she was trying hard to ignore, scowled at her. "Haven't you ever heard of a gun safe?"

"I had no way of knowing Derrick would be poking around and find a weapon. I didn't even know it was there myself!"

"Well, it is." He yanked the rifle from Derrick and shoved the offensive weapon into her hands. "Deal with it. He was poaching on my property."

"Poaching?" Would the fun never end? "He shot something?"

Quinn hiked a diabolical eyebrow. "Want me to file charges?"

She looked at him full on now, fighting down the panic of having him in her space. Either he didn't remember her or he didn't kiss and tell. One was a check in the positive column and the other wasn't. She didn't know which she preferred—hating that he didn't remember at all or admiring him for his respectful silence in front of the boy.

How old was he now? Thirty-four? Thirty-six? He was still gorgeous—sandy brown hair tipped in gold, hazel eyes and strong, athletic body—though lines bisected his forehead as if his problems had taken a toll. She squelched the pinch of pity. He'd been a player on and off the football field. He didn't deserve her sympathy.

"I assure you, this will not happen again." She hoped she could keep that promise.

She grabbed Derrick by the upper arm and propelled him toward the porch.

Quinn didn't take the hint. He followed. "I'm not done with him. Or with you."

"If you're pressing charges, do it, but leave us alone." *Just go away.*

She opened the door, gave Derrick her meanest look, willing him inside before this situation got worse.

A powerful left hand clamped on the screen door. "He could have been hurt. Someone with no gun experience in the woods this time of year is asking for trouble."

Derrick, who never knew when to shut up, cast a derisive glance at Quinn's bent right arm. "Is that what happened to you?"

Both adults froze. Gena lifted her gaze to Quinn's face, which was suddenly as dark and empty as midnight.

He swallowed. "As a matter of fact, yes. I was stupid."

"Well, I'm not. So bug off."

"Derrick!" Gena, aching a little for the man she'd vowed to despise, entered the house and gingerly settled the rifle in a corner. Quinn followed as if he'd been invited. Which he definitely had not been.

"I'm going to my room."

"No, we're going to talk about this. Sit." She pointed to the couch.

Rolling his eyes, Derrick slumped onto the cushions and crossed his arms.

To Quinn, she said, "I apologize for any problem he caused. Thank you for bringing him home. I'll handle it from here."

Her heart was hammering like a woodpecker against her rib cage. She wanted Quinn to go. Even if he didn't remember, she did.

His hair glistening from the mist, Quinn stood in her living room bunched inside his jacket looking as blustery as the weather.

"Has he had a hunter education course?"

Derrick's education was neither Quinn's business nor his problem. "Tell me where you live so I can be sure he doesn't return."

"A fishing cabin about a mile west."

She nodded. "I know the place. I thought it was empty."

"I thought the same about this house," he said with a quick glance around her cozy living room. "Satterfield place, wasn't it?"

"My grandparents' house. Yes." She waited to see if he made the connection. He didn't. Nervous, uncertain, she patted her hands together and said with only the slightest venom, "Well, now that we know each of us is out here, we can be careful not to cross paths again."

Very, very careful.

Quinn frowned and didn't seem the least inclined to leave. "I don't like poachers. If the boy is going to hunt, he needs a license and you need to teach him to obey trespassing laws."

Gena's face tightened. "He's not your concern, Mr. Buchanon."

"He was today." He squinted at her. "Do I know you?"

Her pulse thumped. "No."

"But you apparently know me."

"Everyone knows the Buchanons." She kept her voice casual. Unlike an invisible bookworm named Gena, the

Buchanons were known to everyone in Gabriel's Crossing. Notwithstanding the four gorgeous sons and three pretty daughters, they owned a construction company and had built half the houses in the town. Maybe more.

"Then I'm at a disadvantage. What's your name?"

Gena hesitated. If they were neighbors, which they clearly were, she couldn't act weird. "Gena Satterfield. This is Derrick."

Derrick glared at both adults with the "I hope you die a painful death" stare.

The tumblers rolled around behind Quinn's eyes. "Satterfield," he mused. "Yeah."

She held her breath.

Finally, he said, "Ken and Anna Satterfield lived here, right? Good folks."

Relief seeped through her. He remembered her grandparents. That was all. Nothing suspicious in that. "Yes. They passed away, and the house was empty for a while until Derrick and I decided to move to the country."

"*You* decided," Derrick said, making his feelings on the subject crystal clear.

Quinn glanced at the sullen boy, holding his gaze steady until Derrick looked down. Gena's blood chilled in her veins. *Go away. Stop looking at him.*

As if he'd heard her thoughts and decided to comply, Quinn turned toward the door. Before stepping outside, he said to Derrick, "Fences are there for a reason. Pay attention or pay the consequences."

He slammed the door behind him.

The living room trembled with the sound for several seconds before Gena pointed a finger at Derrick. "You are not *ever* to go anywhere near that man or his property again. Got it?"

He made a noise in the back of his throat and rolled his eyes. And Gena could only pray he listened.

Chapter Two

Quinn didn't expect to see the kid again, but even as he stoked the fireplace the next day and contemplated breakfast, he couldn't help thinking about the surly boy with the soft blue eyes and his pretty, if hostile, mother.

He hadn't slept much last night, more because of the incident and the unexpected meeting than the pain in his arm. He wasn't complaining.

The boy, Derrick, who was probably eleven or twelve going on seventeen, had a chip on his shoulder as big as Alaska, and Quinn vaguely remembered Gena Satterfield from the old days. She'd been an underclassman, kind of nerdy, and hadn't run in his circles. He remembered her sister better. A lot better. He'd made a point not to share that information with Gena.

But Gena wasn't nerdy anymore. She had grown up to be quite the looker—pale skin, round cheeks, cute nose and wavy blond hair to her shoulders. He'd nearly swallowed his tongue when she'd come charging out the door in fuzzy slippers and a baggy University of Texas sweatshirt like some warrior woman to protect her offspring. It had been a long time since he'd had that kind of visceral response to a woman, especially an angry one.

He smiled a little, the curve of lips feeling unnatural.

Mom said he didn't smile enough anymore. Maybe so. He couldn't think of much to smile about, but Gena Satterfield had both irritated and amused him.

She was a doctor or nurse or something medical. Unlike the rest of his family, he didn't pay much attention to Gabriel's Crossing society, but when she'd first moved back to Gabriel's Crossing, the newspaper had carried an article about her, the former resident come back as a primary care practitioner. Nurse practitioner—that was it. He remembered now. She worked with Dr. Ramos.

What he hadn't known was that she'd moved into the old Satterfield place. He didn't notice much of anything anymore. But last night he'd noticed her.

He jabbed the poker at the recalcitrant embers, stirring to get a fire going. Recalcitrant, like the boy.

He'd put the fear in the kid during the ride home. Or he'd tried to. Derrick was a tough nut to crack, a city boy, who looked down his nose at small towns and country people. But he'd been fascinated by the gun. How he'd known about weaponry worried Quinn. City boys had no use for a hunting rifle, but Derrick had some basic knowledge. Enough to fire a lethal weapon. Not good. If the kid was going to handle a gun, he needed to learn to do it properly, to respect the seriousness and responsibility that came with the knowledge. Even then, accidents happened.

He rubbed at his arm, then tossed a log onto the embers and left the fireplace to do its thing while he rummaged up some breakfast.

Derrick Satterfield was not his problem. Not unless the surly kid stepped foot on his three hundred acres again.

When he reached inside the refrigerator, his hand trembled. He folded his fingers into his palms and tried to think of anything except the one thing that eased the gnawing in his gut and the hand shakes.

Maybe a run along the river. He grabbed the milk and poured a glass, then remembered the cat locked in his shed.

With a sigh, he poured a bowl of milk, warmed it in the nuker, donned his coat and hustled across the cedar-stabbed yard. As his arm had predicted, a very thin sheet of ice coated the world, glistening in the intense morning sun. Like back-lit crystals, the ice was beautiful, though damaging to the trees.

"Okay, lady, rise and shine. Today's the day you hit the road. Drink your milk and g—" He stopped in the doorway. He should have expected this. "I told you no kittens."

The tuxedo face glared up at him as her body heaved. Two damp babies, half-naked, lay on the towels. More, apparently, were to come.

He set the milk down on the floor. "Guess you're not interested in this right now."

A third kitten slipped onto the towels. The first two had begun to squirm and make small mewing noises, their eyes tight and faces squinched. The mother gave each a nudge and then went back to tending the newest in her brood.

"Cool. She's having kittens."

At the unexpected voice, Quinn startled and bumped his head on the low doorway as he backed out of the shed. As soon as he saw the speaker, he frowned his meanest scowl.

"What are you doing over here? I told you—"

"I don't have to do what you say. Her, either." Derrick shoved his hands deeper into the pockets of a blue unzipped parka. Beneath, he wore a black sweatshirt with the hood pulled over his forehead. He looked like an inner-city gangster, which was probably his intent.

"I could call the sheriff and have you charged with trespassing."

The threat had no effect on the dark-haired boy. "I know who you are."

Quinn tensed. "Yeah?"

"Yeah. Some hotshot quarterback who got himself shot and ruined his chances at the NFL."

The cold morning air chilled Quinn's breath and set the pain into motion. He squeezed his upper arm. "Where'd you hear that?"

"Dude." Derrick slouched his shoulders and gave off his best you're-so-stupid attitude. "Don't you know about the internet?"

"You looked me up?"

"So? I was bored."

"You got a smart mouth, you know that?"

"I hate this place. She never should have brought me here."

"Why did she?"

The kid went silent, his mouth broody.

Trouble. Derrick must have been in trouble. "Where did you live before?"

"Houston. It's way better than this..." pale blue eyes gazed around at the vast woods and emptiness "...this squirrel-infested backwoods dump."

Quinn arched an eyebrow, shooting back as much venom as Derrick had aimed at him. "Afraid of the woods? Scared of the dark? Nervous when a coyote howls?"

"I'm not afraid of anything."

No, he was terrified. Of life, of the new, unfamiliar environment, of looking soft. So many fears swam around in the kid's head it was a wonder his ears didn't flood. Quinn suffered an unwanted twinge of compassion. "We're all scared of something."

Derrick huddled deeper inside his hoodie. His ears and nose were red, his breath gray.

"Does she know you're over here?"

"What do you think?"

"I think you should go home. Get off my land and quit giving her such a hard time."

From inside the shed came a chorus of plaintive mews. Derrick straightened, his attention riveted on the dim interior. "She had another one."

"You like cats?"

"Not much."

"Me, either."

"Look at 'em." Derrick leaned inside. "They're so little."

Quinn sighed. "Yeah."

"It's cold out here."

He wasn't asking the kid inside. No way. He didn't want people here. No one. Certainly not seventy-five pounds of trouble. "Get in the truck. I'll drive you home."

"Nah. I can walk. Nothing else to do out here." But he made no motion to leave. With his eyes still on the kittens, he kicked his toe against the side of the shed. Ice chipped off. "Were you as good as they say you were?"

Quinn snorted and avoided the kid's probing gaze. "Too long ago to remember."

"A guy doesn't forget stuff like that."

He was right about that. Some things hurt forever. "Doesn't matter now. I got work to do. Go home."

Quinn spun away from the shed, the cats, the kid and the memories and stomped back to the house, ice cracking underfoot. His boots sounded like thunder on the hollow porch.

To his relief, Derrick didn't follow. He didn't even turn around. Instead he stepped inside the shed and shut the door.

Quinn blew out a hard sigh. The kid needed to learn two things: obedience and respect.

He went inside the house, warm now that the logs had caught and burned brightly, and tried to remember where he'd put his phone. After a five-minute search, he found it, battery dead, under a stack of blueprints. Most of the

time, he left it turned off. Service was spotty anyway. If he
wanted to speak to someone, he'd call them—a rare event.

The practice drove his family crazy.

He plugged in the charger and called Information for
Gena Satterfield's number and wasn't surprised to dis-
cover she had a landline. Cell phones worked when they
wanted to and in her profession, effective communication
was probably requisite.

He punched in the number, and when she answered
in her smooth-as-silk, professional voice, he ignored the
quiver in his belly to say, "Derrick's at my house again.
Come get him before I call the sheriff."

Gena fumed all the way down the twisty, bumpy trail
that passed for sections of road between her house and the
old hunting cabin on the river. She couldn't decide who
irritated her most, Derrick or Quinn.

Derrick had been curled up under his covers when she'd
looked in earlier. At least, she'd thought he had been. She'd
let him sleep late this Sunday morning, not in the mood
to fight with him about going to church. She didn't like to
miss services but she had paperwork and dictation to catch
up on anyway. The Lord knew and understood her schedule. She couldn't always attend services, but she never
forgot her faith.

At the corner, she slowed the red SUV and tried to remember exactly how to access the cabin. She hadn't been
there since the last time she and Renae had spent the summer with Nana and Papa. She and her sister had been into
photography that summer. Somewhere she still had the
pictures they'd taken, including shots of the abandoned
hunter's cabin. She couldn't imagine anyone living in the
ramshackle structure, but Quinn came from a construction family. He could fix whatever was broken.

This morning was a photographer's dream, and a desire to revisit the old hobby curled upward in her thoughts. Though the roads were mostly clear and the puddles of ice easily cracked beneath her wheels, the grass and trees sparkled in the sun like diamonds. By midmorning, the beauty would be melted away.

She drove toward the river, invisible from here because of the thick trees, and spotted chimney smoke. In minutes, she funneled through a tunnel of trees that parted like the Red Sea in front of the cabin. The house didn't look much better than it had when she was a teenager.

She slammed out of the now-dirty red Xterra and, careful on the ice-encrusted grass, made her way to Quinn's door. He opened it before she could pound her fist on the wall in frustration.

Her breath caught. He looked tired or maybe ill, his hazel-green eyes circled with fatigue and his mouth pinched with lines of something that to her expert observation appeared to be pain. But he still took a woman's breath. A foolish woman.

"Are you all right?" Her profession kicked in even when she didn't want it to.

He blinked, clearly surprised at the question. "Why?"

This wasn't her business. "Never mind. Where's Derrick?"

Quinn motioned toward a small unpainted building to the left of the house.

"You locked him in a shed?" she asked, horrified.

Quinn snorted. His eyes, so tired before, lit with wry amusement. "I didn't think of that or I would have. Maybe you should try it."

He was joking. He had to be. "What's he doing out there?"

"Go see for yourself." He slammed the door in her face.

Gena stared at the peeling front door. The friendly, smiling young Quinn who could charm the spots off a leopard was now a snarly, moody recluse.

"Well, fine."

She straightened her shoulders and started across the leaf-covered patch of yard. It was better this way. The less she saw of Quinn, the safer her secret. She refused to let him upset her. She wasn't the shy, aching teenager anymore who thought he'd hung the moon.

The cabin door opened behind her. Gena heard footsteps. She tensed and glanced over one shoulder. Quinn was coming her way, shrugging into a coat.

"I'll get him and go," she said. "No need to come out."

Quinn kept right on walking. Sun shot gold through his hair and haloed his head, though he'd never been choir boy material. An amicable guy, but hardly perfect. Except in the looks department. He was still broad shouldered and built like an inverted wedge, a man women noticed. Time might have changed his personality but not his good looks and charisma.

Gena jerked her attention away. No matter how pretty he was, pretty is as pretty does.

She grabbed the wobbly shed handle and yanked, relieved when it didn't fall off in her hand. Derrick was *so* grounded.

"Derrick, get in the…" At the sight before her, the words died in her throat unspoken. Her cranky, surly nephew who didn't seem to care about anything at all these days sat cross-legged on the bare floor while a mother cat licked milk from his fingertips. Nestled around the black-and-white cat was a wad of brand-new baby kittens.

Derrick raised a rapt face. "She had babies. I watched."

Gena went to her haunches. "How many?"

"Four. She's really tired now." He sounded vulnerable and sweet like the loving little boy he'd once been.

"I expect so." She stroked a finger across the mother

cat's head. The animal seemed friendly. The big surprise to her was that Quinn Buchanon would own a cat. An attack-trained Rottweiler, yes. But a cat?

She looked up at the bewildering man standing inside the door. Had she misjudged him?

He was watching her. Not Derrick or the cats but her. For ten seconds their eyes held. Gena suffered a dozen conflicting emotions—completely unwanted attraction and a desire to know the man behind the haggard face and bent, scarred arm. Remembrance of who he'd once been, of what he'd done. Fear that he would learn the truth and hurt Derrick more. The last thought tugged her focus back to the boy.

"We should go. I have work to catch up on and you have homework for tomorrow."

The sweet expression disappeared so fast she thought she'd imagined it. "I hate school."

Big news. He said those same words every day. "Derrick…"

Quinn squatted beside her; the scent of wood smoke and cold air circled around him. To Derrick he said, his voice almost gentle, "Don't worry about the kittens. They'll be okay."

Derrick's pale eyes flashed to Quinn. He tried to appear nonchalant but Gena saw what she'd missed, what Quinn had seen. The boy had always had a soft spot for animals, but she'd thought it had disappeared along with the rest of his sweet nature.

"The mother knows what to do," she said. "She'll care for them."

"But they can't see. Their eyes are glued shut. What if they get too far away from her?"

"She'll bring them back." To prove the point, Quinn reached into the box and gently lifted a tiny kitten by the scruff, moving it slightly away from the mama. It mewed.

Instantly, the mother cat rose to bring the kitten back with the others and gave it a rough-tongued lick for good measure.

"Oh." Derrick swiped a sleeve over his nose and sniffed. "Dumb cats."

Gena felt a smile coming on. Without intending to, she glanced at Quinn and saw his eyes spark, too.

Suddenly afraid, she scrambled to her feet. "Let's go. We promised Mr. Buchanon to stay away from here."

"*You* promised. I didn't."

The mulish attitude was back.

"You don't get a say in this, kid. I'm the boss around here." Quinn's voice was casual but made of steel as he rose to his full and impressive height. What was he? Like six-five or something?

"But if you behave yourself, you can come back another time to see the kittens. And I won't call the sheriff."

Derrick's shoulders relaxed the slightest bit. "Yeah?"

"No!" Gena shoved the shed door open, pulse thrumming. The bare wood slammed against the wall, ripping the gray morning.

Derrick was giving her heart trouble. At this rate, she'd be in cardiac arrest before her next birthday. "You can't come here again. I've already told you that, but if you don't argue, I'll ground you from the computer for only two days."

"That's stupid," he groused, but exited the well house and stomped across the frozen ground toward the SUV.

Gena sighed, aware that she'd won one battle but lost another. Derrick seemed to slip further away all the time. No matter what she did, he resented it.

Quinn came up beside her. She didn't look at him, didn't trust herself to look into his weary face and feel things that weren't allowed. He was the enemy of all she held dear, and she'd do well to remember it.

"Has he always been this belligerent?"

"No." Gena stared at the frozen ground, saw the gleam of ice that would soon melt away. If only problems would do the same. "He used to be the sweetest boy, the happy, cuddly kid who adored me."

Back when she hadn't been the boss. Back when Renae— She shut the door on the useless thought. She'd chosen this life for Renae's sake, and she refused to regret the decision.

Without another word or glance, she strode to the SUV and drove away. Derrick simply could not come back to this place. Ever.

Chapter Three

Two weeks passed, but Quinn knew he hadn't seen the last of the troublesome neighbors. There was daily evidence that Derrick had snuck into the well house to see the kittens. He figured Gena didn't know. Otherwise, why the secrecy?

This morning an opened but uneaten can of tuna was stashed in one dark corner of the shed. He'd smelled it the minute he'd opened the door.

Now at work inside the offices of Buchanon Construction, Quinn frowned at the sets of blueprints on his desk. His office was in the back of the warehouse, a quieter space than the front desks ruled by two of his sisters. Here he could work in peace and hang out with the coffeemaker. And wonder about his unexpected neighbors.

He refused to worry that the mother cat hadn't been in the shed this morning. Or last night, for that matter. She came and went as she pleased. They weren't his cats. He didn't like cats.

But he wasn't an ogre, either, contrary to popular opinion. He'd put a heating pad under the babies, turned to low like the internet said, to keep them warm. While he cleaned out the box and set up the heating pad, he'd put each kitten inside his zippered jacket, next to his warm skin. They were soft as down, and now that their eyes were squinted open, they were kind of cute.

"We missed you yesterday." His brother Brady, the company's manager and his closest sibling in age, propped a hip on the edge of his desk. As youths they'd been constant companions but after the accident that destroyed his throwing arm, Brady continued to play college football while Quinn was left behind to deal with surgeries and rehab and pain. Their lives had gone in separate directions, certainly not the direction he'd intended, and only in the last year had they intersected again. Brady didn't know all he'd gone through in Dallas. Quinn didn't want anybody to know.

He pretended to study the diagrams. "I was busy."

"Yeah? Doing what?"

"Stuff."

Brady barked a laugh. "You missed a good basketball game. The Mavericks beat the Thunder in OT."

Yes, and his mother probably made chili or pot roast and the siblings stocked the kitchen with chips, dips and other snacks. Sunday afternoons were a tradition at the Buchanon house. Everyone came to watch a game. It didn't matter what kind of game. Football was the favorite, but they watched basketball, baseball, anything that gave them an excuse to gather after church and yell at the TV—all in fun, of course. He missed those times with his family, but they didn't understand how hard it was for him to be there.

He'd fallen off the proverbial wagon last night. Not as completely as he had in the past but enough to shame him.

He did all right at work. Rigidly, every day, he brought exactly two pain pills to the office. The prescribed amount. Two and only two to get him through the day.

Nights were murder. Last night the pain had won.

He rubbed his shoulder and swallowed the thick, nasty taste of failure. "Maybe next week."

"That's what you've said every week since last Christmas. We miss you, brother." Brady's voice softened. "*I* miss you."

A lump rose in Quinn's throat. "Yeah, well…" What could he say? He loved Brady. Loved his family. But he was lousy company, unfit to be part of the wholesome Buchanon clan until he defeated the monster living inside him.

"Want to talk about it?"

Startled, he glanced up. "About what?"

No way Brady could know the truth. Quinn had been too careful.

"Whatever it is that's keeping you away."

The air hummed with expectation. Brady wanted an answer. Quinn wasn't giving him one.

Finding a smirk, he said, "You're too busy romancing Abby to miss me."

Brady got a besotted grin on his face. "I can't wait to marry that woman. She's something special."

Quinn softened. His brother was happy. Regardless of the problems plaguing Buchanon Construction and a fire that had destroyed his Christmas home-makeover project, Brady had fallen in love with the recipient. Waitress Abby Webster and her little girl had filled the lonely spot in Brady and become as much a part of the family as if they'd always been there. "I'm happy for you, Brady."

"You should think about finding a good woman for yourself."

A pair of angry green eyes flashed through his head. Irritated, he said, "Don't want one."

"Who are you kidding? You love women. And they love you."

"That was a long time ago. I'm not that guy anymore."

"Maybe that's not such a bad thing," Brady said quietly.

"Mom said you had a run-in with the new nurse practitioner. What happened?"

"Long story. She's got this kid. Pain in the neck. I caught the little twerp hunting on my property. And there's this cat."

"You have a cat?"

He scowled. "No, I don't have a cat. I don't like cats. But a pregnant mama had kittens in my well house a couple of weeks ago. What was I supposed to do? Toss them in the river?"

"What does this have to do with Gena Satterfield?"

"Nothing." He ran an irritated hand through his hair. "Like I said, she's got this kid. He's infatuated with the kittens."

"Didn't you date her sister? Renae, wasn't it?"

Quinn huffed. "Yeah."

"I wonder where she is now."

"A rhetorical question, I hope. I certainly don't know." But he'd wondered plenty of times.

Bothered, he crossed to the coffeemaker. One of the twins, Sawyer probably, had arrived early and filled the Bunn maker to capacity. Buchanons imbibed massive amounts of coffee.

Talk of Gena or Derrick or, heaven forbid, Renae, set his nerves on edge.

"Her kid's named Derrick." He didn't know why he'd said that. Maybe because he'd been thinking about the Satterfields too much. Gena had a son but there was no man in her life. He'd figured that much out. He'd asked around. Carefully. Subtly. A man needed to know who his neighbors were, especially when they trespassed with regularity.

And yeah, he was curious about her and the guy she'd loved enough to have a son with. A jerk, apparently. Maybe his absence was the reason Derrick was so angry.

"Whose kid?" Brady asked. "Renae's?"

"No, meathead, Gena's." He poured two cups and handed one to Brady.

"You didn't date her, too, did you?"

Quinn barked a rusty laugh. "No."

"I had an appointment with Dr. Ramos last week, routine stuff, and ran into Gena in the hallway." Brady lifted an eyebrow. "Nice. Pretty, too."

Yeah, he'd noticed. Maybe not the nice part but the pretty for certain.

He pretended to study the steam rising from his mug. "Want me to tell Abby about your sudden interest in the new nurse practitioner?"

"I'm talking about you, dunce cap." Brady shook his head in dismay. "From what I hear, she's still single, and obviously she's smart and successful. Plus, she lives close enough for the two of you to get acquainted."

Quinn offered a scowl. "I don't like people in my space."

"Suit yourself, bro." Brady lifted a hand in dismissal.

"She doesn't like me."

Brady dropped his hand and frowned. "No vibes?"

"None." At least not from her direction. His vibes had done a few calisthenics. Maybe a couple of wind sprints.

"The old Buchanon charm didn't work?"

His charm had been in his right arm. Women didn't care about the real Quinn. They cared about the prestige of being seen with the nation's top college quarterback, destined for the big time and lots of money, not about a damaged man who struggled to get through every day and night without falling down the rabbit hole. Even now, his arm ached and he wished for the bottle of painkillers waiting on the counter at the cabin.

"Are you going to work today or harass me about my single status?"

"Both." Brady plunked the half-empty mug on the long

counter that ran behind Quinn's desk. "I need some minor tweaks to the Robinson house."

"Figures. Let me pull those up." He rotated his computer screen and typed in the project name. "The mama was gone this morning."

"Our mama? Where did she go? I thought she was helping Charity fluff the resale house on Hannah Street."

Quinn poked his brother's arm with the side of his fist. "Not *our* mama. The mama cat. She wasn't there last night, either."

"Kittens still there?"

"She didn't move them, if that's what you're thinking. She's gone. The kittens aren't."

"That doesn't sound good." Brady pinched his upper lip. "You've got coyotes out your way. What are you going to do if she doesn't return?"

Quinn squeezed his aching biceps. If it wasn't one problem, it was another.

"I have no idea."

When he arrived home that evening, the sun was low in the west and shadowy tree fingers gripped the shed. He hoped the mother cat had returned. He'd even stopped at the IGA and picked up a few cans of cat food for her. Not that he wanted her sticking around once the kittens were old enough to travel, but she needed her strength to see them to adolescence.

He dumped the bag of groceries on the counter along with a foil-wrapped casserole his mother had brought to the office. He glanced at the bottle of painkillers sitting harmlessly next to the sugar bowl. He picked them up and read the warning label for the thousandth time.

"'May be habit-forming.'" He spat a cheerless laugh. "No kidding."

The crawly craving started up. Just one more. Just one

extra pill and his arm would stop aching and he wouldn't have to think so much about all he'd lost. His mind would slide away into that peaceful place where nothing hurt, not even his soul, and...

He slammed the plastic container onto the counter and, heart pounding, jogged out into the cold, across the yard and to the shed.

Derrick was already there. He held a baby kitten in each hand.

Quinn's heart sunk lower than the setting sun. The mama was nowhere in sight. Four babies writhed and cried as if they hadn't eaten all day.

"Something's wrong with them," Derrick said, his usually sullen face creased in worry.

"The mama wasn't here this morning."

"I know."

Quinn shot him a quick look. "Last night, either."

"I didn't think she'd run off like that."

"Something must have happened to her. She wouldn't leave them on purpose. She's a good mama. Like yours."

Derrick's expression turned belligerent. "What would you know about it?"

"Not a thing." He didn't know why he wanted to butt into the shaky relationship between Derrick and Gena. They were not his problem. These cats were. Sort of.

Quinn hunkered down beside the box and lifted one of the kittens, a solid white puffball. Her mouth opened in a display of pointed teeth, pink gums and desperation. She wailed, loud and strong.

Awkwardly, he stroked her head and back. "Shh. Don't cry, little one. Shh."

"You really think the mama's gone for good?" Derrick looked as sad as if they were orphaned humans instead of stray cats.

"Whether she is or not, the fact remains, these kittens won't survive without her much longer."

"You got a computer?"

"Why?"

Derrick slumped and shook his head in disgust. "Dude. Haven't you ever heard of research? Somebody knows what to do. Google it."

The kid was likely right, but company in his cabin was not Quinn's favorite thing.

He carefully replaced the crying kitten, sympathy tugging at him. They were pitiful little creatures. He weighed their struggle against his own and gave in. "My laptop's on the table inside."

Derrick didn't hesitate. With a gentle hand that belied his don't-care attitude, he settled the kittens onto the warm pad, murmured reassurances and rose. "Let's go. They're starving."

"Maybe Gena would know what to do."

As he shuffled to the doorway, Derrick glanced to one side, eyes avoiding Quinn's. "I doubt it."

"She doesn't know you're here, does she?"

The kid looked up and scoffed. "Are you kidding me? She'd ground me for years."

"I must have made a great impression on her." He'd been less than friendly, which he figured was justifiable. They'd trespassed. Not him. But Gena's attitude rankled him. He didn't want people hanging around, but he wasn't Jack the Ripper, either.

"She gets all twitchy and weird when I mention your name." The kid shoved his hands into the pouch of his hoodie. "Did you, like, know each other back in the old days or something?"

The old days. Right.

Quinn led the way out of the shed and took care to secure the rickety latch. Darkness blanketed the yard except for the pale light from a white moon. The kid shouldn't be here this late. Home was a long walk in the cold and dark. "We both attended Gabriel's Crossing High School but didn't run in the same circles."

"Yeah, you were Mr. Big Shot. She was nobody."

Quinn cut the kid a sharp look. "Did Gena tell you that?"

"She didn't have to. Your picture is plastered in the trophy cases and on all kinds of plaques. Hers isn't."

A hot pain slid up Quinn's elbow and into his shoulder. "Still?"

"Yeah. Kind of weird."

It sure was.

Quinn fell silent. Old memories made for long nights. Forget the past. Move on.

Inside the house, he turned his attention to the kittens. "Laptop's there. Have at it."

The boy lifted the lid and said in a reverent tone, "Touch screen. Sweet."

"I'm an architect. High tech comes in handy."

Derrick's fingers raced over the keyboard. "You do graphics and stuff?"

"Yeah. *Stuff.* Lots and lots of stuff."

"Plenty of sites about orphaned kittens." The boy clicked on one of them.

Quinn leaned over his shoulder to watch. In minutes, they'd learned the rudiments of caring for the kittens. "Looks like we'll need milk replacer from the vet. Too late for that tonight."

"We can try this homemade stuff." Derrick pointed at the screen and rattled off the list of ingredients.

"I have the eggs but not the condensed milk."

"We could go to the store." Derrick's voice was hopeful, though his expression said he expected Quinn to turn him down.

"You need to go home." His mom would be getting worried by now.

"And let the kittens die?" Derrick slammed out of the chair in a fury, fists tight at his side. "Creep. If you won't take me to town, I'll walk."

"Whoa. Whoa. Calm down there, tiger. Call home for permission first. I don't want her on my case."

Derrick didn't ease off. "That makes two of us."

Quinn tried to remember where he'd left his cell. "Phone's in the truck. Be right back."

As he stepped outside, Gena's SUV broke through his protective line of trees. She jerked to a stop next to his pickup and stormed out, slamming the door with vehemence.

"Is Derrick over here?"

No use getting testy with him. He hadn't invited the little twerp. "In the house."

She shot him a hard glance and marched to the front door. She waited there in her jaunty knitted cap with her arms crossed over a blue coat as if unsure whether to barge into his cabin or wait for his permission. Feeling obstinate, he didn't give it. Instead he took his sweet time finding his cell phone, all the while watching her from the corner of his eye.

She was steamed, whether at him or Derrick or both, he couldn't say and didn't care. They were trouble. Pains in the neck. He didn't need them or their intrusion on his peace and quiet.

He forced a leisurely stroll across his own front yard. The air seeped through his shirtsleeves, but he refused to rush. She made him want to get under her skin. "You know anything about feeding orphaned kittens?"

She uncrossed her arms, pursed pink lips easing open. "Did something happen to the mother?"

"Appears so." He reached the porch and pushed open

the door, motioning her inside. She crossed in front of him and he was surprised that she smelled nice, not like the antiseptic medical scent he'd expected. Something subtle, spicy and warm wrapped around his senses.

She was average height, reaching him about chin high. And beneath her coat she wore turquoise scrubs, a good color with her green eyes.

He gave an inner laugh. Stupid thought process. What did he care about the color of her eyes? He just wanted her and her little twerp out of his house.

Gena strode directly to Derrick. "You could have left a note."

"You knew where to look."

Derrick shrugged her off and turned back to the laptop. Gena shifted on her Crocs, uncertain. She wasn't assertive enough with the kid. She let him get away with too much.

The room pulsed with silence, not that Quinn minded. He liked quiet. The woman and boy weren't his concern.

He moved to the fireplace, crouching to add a log. Behind him Gena said something to Derrick about the kittens and they discussed the milk replacer.

He heard her say, "They'll need to be fed at least every six hours."

"I can do it. I'll come before school and right after. I'll even come in the middle of the night."

Quinn pivoted around, quiet and watching.

Gena was shaking her blond head. "No."

"Why not?"

"Derrick, come on, be sensible. You have school and I have work."

"It would only be for a little while." His expression went from sullen to impassioned. "I can't let them starve to death!"

She seemed to contemplate the determined, disobedient

kid along with the problems inherent with feeding animals orphaned this young.

"I suppose we could take them home with us. That's a better solution anyway. Then you won't be over here bothering Quinn."

"Can we?"

Quinn pushed up and away from the fireplace. "No."

Both woman and boy turned to stare at him. "Why not?"

He hitched a shoulder, feeling obstinate. What right did she have to come into his house and dictate what became of the animals in his shed? "My cats."

"You said they were strays."

"They were until they took up residence in my shed." What was he doing? Let her take them. Be rid of them. Be rid of her and her sulky kid. Get back to normal. Alone. The way he liked. "They stay."

"Are you going to feed them?"

"We'll work out a schedule."

"I don't want Derrick over here."

"Why not?" That was what was bugging him most. Now that he'd offered the invitation, he didn't appreciate her attitude. As if he was some kind of evil influence on children. He was the one making the sacrifice by letting Derrick invade his private sanctuary.

She parked a hand on one hip. "You're unbelievable, you know that? First you threaten to call the sheriff if he steps foot on your land, and now you're asking me to let him come here several times a day."

She was really cute when she got fired up. Like a bunny rabbit on a rampage. He wanted to laugh. For the first time in a long time, he was sparring with a woman who attracted him. He even wanted to make her like him. But he was rusty in the charm department.

He knew he should give in and let her take the kittens. The last thing he needed was to have a troubled boy hanging around for two or three weeks. If the kid followed through. Which he probably wouldn't.

"The responsibility would be good for him."

"Come on, Gena," Derrick wheedled. "It'll only be for a week or two."

Gena? Why would her kid call her by her first name? Disrespect?

The little twerp needed his head thumped.

She put her hand on the boy's shoulder and massaged. "Honey, I know you're worried about the kittens, but—"

Derrick yanked away, his face closed and his breath coming fast and short. "But what? You're not going to let me do it because you don't like Quinn?"

Quinn raised both eyebrows and pinned her with a stare. Her cheeks reddened.

"There are some things you have to trust me on. This is one of them." She shot Quinn a snarky look. "The cats belong to Quinn. *He* can take care of them. Now get in the car and let's go home."

Derrick's face darkened. His mouth was tight, his eyes laser hot. "I don't have to do what you say. You're not my mother. Stop trying to be."

Gena's face went whiter than wall plaster. Her pale green eyes flashed toward Quinn. "Derrick!"

Shocked, confused and feeling stupid, Quinn looked from woman to boy and back to the woman.

She wasn't his mother? Then who was?

Chapter Four

Gena's heart was pushing through her chest. Any minute now, she'd collapse dead on Quinn Buchanon's rough wooden floor.

If she was fortunate. Which today she was not.

Quinn stared squint-eyed at her, the way he must have stared down offensive linemen back in the golden days. Looking angry and dangerous, he awaited an explanation.

"She's my aunt," Derrick said with a sneer. "Good for me."

Quinn's chilly gaze swung to the boy. "Your aunt."

"Yeah. Are you deaf? What did you think? That she was my mom or something?"

Thanks for the vote of confidence, Derrick.

Mouth tight, Quinn pointed a warning at Derrick before those cold eyes swung back to her. She held them with her own green ones, fighting the rising panic, blustering her way through the awkward situation. She'd worked in trauma. She didn't rattle easily.

"His mother died. Not that it's any of your business."

Quinn lifted both hands. "Right. Not my business *at all.*"

Gena waited for the flicker of recognition that never

came. If he remembered Renae, he didn't make the connection.

Derrick slumped to one hip. "So are you gonna let me take care of the kittens or not?"

"Not," she managed. "And don't give me any more nonsense. My patience is gone."

Kittens or not, she was done here. *Done.*

Without waiting to see if her nephew would follow, Gena escaped Quinn's dangerous stare before the world caved in.

Quinn squinted at the clock next to his bunk. Midnight. He'd slept two whole hours, as if his body wanted to wake and torment him for the remaining two. His arm ached, nothing new there, and sleep wouldn't come again until after the medication. He shoved out of the bed and dressed in sweats. The kittens would be hungry soon and he didn't expect Derrick to show, not after the fiasco this afternoon.

He felt misled and shouldn't. He wasn't exactly social, so he had no reason to know through the grapevine that Derrick was Gena's nephew.

Which meant Renae was the little twerp's mother.

It hit him then, like a gunshot. Renae was dead.

"Whoa." Quinn scrubbed a hand over his scruffy jaw and stood stock-still for several seconds. Renae was dead. No wonder the kid was angry.

He padded on the cold wooden floor into the kitchen to prepare for the kittens' feeding.

He wanted to ask Gena what had happened, but she would say it wasn't his business.

It wasn't. He didn't want it to be. In fact, he hoped he never saw either of his problematic neighbors again. He didn't want people infringing on his privacy and blundering around on his land. He'd bought three hundred acres of remote nothing for a reason. To be alone.

Alone was the only way to be until he got the monster off his back.

With the four tiny bottles of warmed milk replacer in his coat, Quinn stepped out into the cold night. Frost lay like a young snow over the grass and bushes, while the moon cast a white, ghostly hue over the shadowy trees and well house.

Winter was not a friend to scar tissue and damaged bone.

The surgical scars started their steady thrum of hot pain, and he whispered a thank-you to the heavens that the kittens would keep him occupied for a while. Anything to block the hunger for another painkiller.

A thin beam of yellow light slanted through the crack in the well-house door.

Quinn blew out a cloudy breath and shook his head.

Was the kid here?

Sure enough, Derrick sat on the floor inside, holding a kitten that sucked greedily at a milk bottle while the other three still in the box yowled in high-pitched desperation.

Quinn ignored the kindness of a boy traipsing through dark woods at midnight to feed motherless kittens. He scowled. "I told you to stay home. I got this one."

"I was awake."

Quinn grunted. So was he.

No point in asking if Gena had given permission. She hadn't. But the kid was her problem, not his. If she let him get away with that kind of disobedience, she'd have to live with the consequences. He had his own problems.

Managing to squeeze his big body into the narrow space opposite Derrick, Quinn scooped two squirming, squalling babies into his left hand while balancing the pair of bottles between the fingers of his right one. Awkward but efficient.

Derrick watched for a second and then looked at his

much smaller palm cradling a single baby. Quinn could tell he wanted to say something but the chip on his shoulder weighed him down.

"Big hands," Quinn muttered, remembering the way a football fit perfectly and wondering why he bothered to make conversation with a pain-in-the-neck boy who should be home in bed.

Derrick's defensive pose softened as curiosity got the better of him. "Can you palm a basketball?"

Quinn jerked a nod. "Haven't in a while, but yeah."

"I wish I could."

"You're still growing." He was a good-sized boy for eleven, tall and lanky and on the verge of adolescence, when his jeans would be shorter every time he put them on. In the next couple of years, he'd grow even taller.

"I like football better anyway."

"Me, too."

The kid snorted. "Obviously." And then surprisingly, "Do you miss playing?"

"Sometimes." All the time.

"You still work out." When Quinn's glance questioned, he pretended to be cool. "I saw your weight set inside."

Except for his arm, Quinn was in the best shape of his life. Rehab and running miles and miles with an addiction chasing you would do that. He punished his body because it had let him down.

When the kitten emptied the bottle, Derrick pressed the now-calm baby against his cheek and stroked its tiny belly with one gentle fingertip. Quinn watched, mesmerized by the boy's tenderness with animals, a tenderness he hid from humans.

Derrick punished humans because they'd let him down. Or maybe he was punishing himself.

Quinn pondered the thought, not wanting this quiet,

warm mood of empathetic companionship springing up in the well house over a box of cats nobody wanted.

But he had to admit a grudging admiration for a kid who would drag himself out of bed in the dark and cold to care for an animal. The action showed something caring and decent about the inner person.

The boy placed his now-fed runt of the litter, a tuxedo like her mother, into the box and gently lifted the final crying baby, a solid black. Quinn's pair, one tuxedo and the other white, nursed contentedly, their tiny paws massaging the nipple as they would their mother.

He and the boy didn't say anything more for a while. From the corner of his eye, Quinn watched the tired face across from him. Derrick was trying so hard to remain tough and aloof, he was about to implode.

"Why are you so mad at her?" he asked softly.

His face, smoothed by the kittens, went sullen again. "What do you care?"

"Just making conversation. She doesn't seem so bad."

A shoulder jerked. "You don't know anything."

"She beat on you?"

Surprised, Derrick's eyes lit in an almost smile but he caught himself in time to scoff. "No."

"Starve you?"

"She's like a doctor or something, man. She wouldn't do that."

"So what's your beef?"

Derrick stared down at the kitten and mumbled, "She shoulda told me."

"Told you what?"

One beat passed. "Nothing."

That's what he got for asking. Nothing.

Quinn removed the bottles from the sated kittens and placed them on the heating pad. Derrick did the same. Neither spoke until they exited the building.

"Get in the truck. I'll drive you home."

"I walked here, didn't I?"

"Suit yourself." Quinn spun and started toward the house. As his foot thudded on the loose porch boards, Derrick said, "Uh, hey, uh."

Quinn stopped but didn't turn. "The name's Quinn."

"Uh, yeah, Quinn. I guess you can drive me home."

A grin wiggled against Quinn's lips. He headed for his Ram. Derrick hopped inside, slammed the door and slumped down in the seat, hood up and hands in his pockets.

They drove in silence down the bumpy trail to the gravel road, shivering deep in their coats until the heater grabbed hold.

The dash clock showed two o'clock. He'd made it, thanks to the cats and the kid. One small victory. One night without regrets.

"You have school tomorrow?"

"Like I can avoid it."

"GC is a pretty good school."

"Nobody likes new kids."

Quinn flicked a glance at him. "Maybe because you have a mountain-sized chip on your shoulder."

"So?" His glare said it all.

So? So plenty of guys could snap you like a number-two pencil, you little twerp.

All he said was, "Be careful or someone will knock it off."

Derrick huffed. "Let 'em try."

"You play sports?"

"Used to. I quit after—" He slid farther down in the seat. Pity welled in Quinn. The dash glow showed a sad kid, not a bad one.

He knew a little about being so sad that you wanted

to disappear and the only emotion you could muster was anger.

The words pressed at the back of Quinn's throat until they fell out in the dark silence. "Lousy, about your mother."

Derrick didn't answer. He turned toward the window and stared out at the black night.

Not your business, Buchanon. You don't need this.

So he shut up. Making conversation with Derrick was like trying to pet a rabid porcupine anyway. What was the point?

At the corner leading to the rear of the Satterfield farm, the kid suddenly came to life. "You can let me out here."

Quinn tapped the brake. "You think she won't find out?"

"You gonna tattle?"

"I'll think about it."

The kid slid to the ground. "Thanks for the ride."

Quinn jerked a nod. "Sleep in. I'll feed them at six."

"I'll be there." Derrick slammed the door and took off in a jog down the road.

Quinn watched the penlight bob across the field and into the backyard and finally disappear into the house before he turned the truck around and drove back to the cabin.

The next day, the Family Medical Clinic was jammed with sick people, and Gena's brain vacillated between medical mode and stressing over Derrick and the untenable situation with her cranky neighbor.

Her sister had been right. Quinn was a player, a user. He didn't even remember.

She ripped off a prescription and handed it to her latest patient, the owner of a local café, The Buttered Biscuit, who'd contracted a mean sinusitis complicated by otitis media.

"I'm prescribing some antibiotics for the infection, Jan. Three times a day for fourteen days. Take all of them, even if you think you feel better. Ear infections can be tricky to clear."

Jan nodded her head miserably, then winced at the pain the movement generated. "I'd eat rocks for a month to get rid of this. I sure don't want it to come back."

Gena smiled. "Smart woman. You can take over-the-counter pain reliever if you need it. Which I'm guessing you do. The same with a decongestant or nasal spray. Call me if you don't see improvement by Friday."

"Thanks, Gena. You're a blessing."

"It wouldn't hurt you to get some rest, let someone else run the café for a few days."

"I feel so awful, I will. Abby can handle it."

Abby. Fiancée to one of the Buchanon boys. As if she needed another reminder of that prominent family today.

Gena opened the exam room door and let the woman pass before going to the sink to wash her hands.

Moving back to Gabriel's Crossing had seemed like the best solution when Derrick began acting out. Here was a familiar place where she knew people and had roots that she could share with him, a place where he could learn small-town values, a place with a mortgage-free home in the country and a medical practice that needed her. Now she wondered if she'd done the right thing.

Maybe she should move back to Houston, away from the danger of Quinn Buchanon.

She scrubbed harder, soaping her wrists, zoned out in thought. Houston didn't have Quinn, but her parents' city had plenty of other worries, especially concerning her nephew.

She loved it here in Gabriel's Crossing, loved living

in Nana and Papa's house with its wonderful memories and quiet woods and pretty yard. Nana had planted something for every season, even winter, when the red berries against deep green holly fed the birds and the spirit. Spring would soon arrive and Nana's lilacs and forsythias would brighten the world.

She didn't want to move again.

Since she'd joined Dr. Ramos last September, her practice had grown rapidly. She loved knowing her patients on a personal basis, seeing them at church and in stores. People liked her personal involvement, her follow-up phone calls, the smart, concerned care she gave. She was a good certified registered nurse practitioner, and she wanted to practice in a rural town where doctors were in short supply. Gabriel's Crossing was perfect. Almost.

Derrick was furious with her about the kittens and had locked himself in his room with his computer, refusing to come out until this morning. Oddly, he'd been up and dressed but his eyes were red rimmed and tired, as if he hadn't slept much.

He worried her out of her mind. And she felt guilty about the baby kittens. Had Quinn fed them? Would he?

Quinn. The biggest problem of all.

Lord, what am I supposed to do? I can't break my promise, but I can't return to Houston. Derrick is better off here in a small town where I can keep a close eye on him. But what if—

Someone tapped on the exam room door. "Gena?"

"Come on in." She glanced up.

Alabama Watts, both nurse and friend, poked her head around the door edge. "Mr. Chard in room three and little Clara Jameson in five are both ready. And Dr. Ramos wants you to take his patients for the next couple of hours. He had an emergency at the hospital."

Gena shut off the water and reached for a paper towel.

She was needed here. Badly.

"Who's first?"

"Mr. Chard. I set up a suture tray. His hand is wrapped in a towel but bleeding through. Chain saw bit him, he said."

"Ouch. Let's go see."

The rest of her day was wildly busy, so by the time she arrived home, the sun had set. She parked the SUV under the carport and opened the side entry door, frowning to see no light glowing from Derrick's room. The bus ran by the house around four. He should have been home three hours ago.

"Derrick?" She tossed her keys and bag on the kitchen counter and went to his room.

The door was shut. She tapped. "Derrick, honey. I'm home."

Nothing.

"Are you hungry?" Wasn't he always?

Still no answer, so she tried the doorknob and found it unlocked. With a deep breath, she stepped into his bedroom. It was empty. His laptop was open and on but dark. His books had been dumped on his unmade bed. If he had homework, he'd likely not done it.

With an exasperated growl, she knew where he'd gone. Quinn's. The kittens.

Wearily, she rubbed at her temples.

She'd been foolish to believe she could avoid anyone in a town this small. Derrick's blatant disregard for her rules meant he was sure to do exactly what she forbade.

As she started out, some gut instinct stopped her. She stared at Derrick's laptop.

She'd not checked his history in a while, and from his weariness this morning, she suspected he'd stayed up late last night trolling the internet. With him out of the house, it was a good time to have a look at his search history without starting another war.

She tapped the touch pad and the screen lit up.

Facebook. *Dandy.* He wasn't old enough to have an account. But when had she been able to stop Derrick from doing something he wanted to do?

She stared at the selfies of the handsome young boy with the sullen mouth and that blasted black hoodie pulled low over his eyes.

With a tap, she refreshed the screen and scrolled, checking out his friends and messages.

The more she read, the colder she got. One "friend" flashed gang signs and puffed on something that looked suspiciously like a marijuana joint. One urged him to hitch his way back to Houston. Another bragged about a "piece" he'd stolen from his old man.

A piece? As in a gun?

"Oh no. Not guns and drugs." She'd thought the shoplifting episode was scary. "He's not even twelve!"

But the young and angry, she knew from her clinic experience in the inner city, were prime targets for gangs and trouble. Derrick was both.

Holding her stomach, she closed the laptop and left the room, reeling. What if he'd read the messages and run away? Houston was miles and miles from Gabriel's Crossing.

Frightened now, Gena grabbed her keys and loped for the Xterra, praying he was at Quinn's place with the kittens. Even there was better than on the road to Houston.

Chapter Five

Quinn stirred the stew pot and breathed in the warming beef-and-tomato scent. Though the calendar had turned a page, the weather remained lousy cold until he wondered if spring would ever come. A pot of stew would last him for days.

He clanged the lid on and went to his work table; the plans he was tweaking for Brady waited. Work and pain. That's all his life amounted to these days.

He rubbed his arm, wishing for relief like always this time of day, when the last painkiller had long since worn off and the hours until the next one loomed long and horrible.

The kid was with the kittens, but Quinn saw no reason to join him. He wasn't in the mood for company.

He'd spotted Derrick coming through the woods as he'd pulled in from work, grumpy as usual after a day of haggling with his workaholic father and brother. The Huckleberry Addition had been problematic since they'd turned the first shovel of dirt. Vandalism, delays, changes.

He focused on the blueprints. Adding an extra bathroom and closet meant an overhaul of the south side. He'd have to give it some thought and run some cost calculations.

The pain crept down his shoulder, flared like hot embers in his bent elbow and spread into his fingers. He opened and closed his hand. He used to do that after a touchdown pass. Flex his fingers, feel the strength that allowed him to throw a ball like a precision torpedo thirty or forty yards past the line of scrimmage. Long, medium or short—no matter the yardage, the Mighty Quinn had been deadly accurate.

These days he couldn't hit a trash can with a paper wad.

Rotten day. Rotten weather. Stinkin' rotten nagging pain.

He glanced at the clock.

Too long. He'd never make it. Why fight the inevitable?

Before he could think too much, he walked the short distance to the sink and opened the brown prescription bottle. One or two? He shook the pills into his hand. Two.

He was going down the tubes anyway. Might as well go without his arm screaming.

Quickly, he washed the pills back with a slug of water. The medication had no more than hit bottom when the shame rushed in.

Failure and shame. Once a month, he drove an hour to refill his prescriptions so no one in Gabriel's Crossing would know their former gridiron hero might have a drug problem.

He was a Christian, or professed to be. Christians weren't supposed to become dependent on painkillers. So where did that leave him?

Defeated, he made his way back to the computer, then to the stove, restless and waiting for relief.

Quinn wondered if Gena had learned about her nephew's trudge through the woods last night.

He should probably tell her, but she didn't seem too eager to communicate, and the kid needed those cats to soften him up.

Or maybe Quinn enjoyed getting under Nurse Gena's skin.

She didn't like him. Even Derrick said so. No big surprise. He wasn't a superstar any longer. After the accident, women had run away from him like cockroaches from a spotlight. Derrick's mother had been one of those fair-weather women. Renae. They'd had something good going—or he'd thought they had—until she learned he was damaged, disabled, a has-been.

"Come on, oxy, do your job."

He flopped on the couch and aimed the remote, scrolling through the satellite until he found elevator music. Tipping his head back, he let his body relax. The pain began to ease and the stress of the day floated away on a river of relief. He knew the relief wouldn't last, but for now it was enough.

As he drifted a bit, waiting for his stew to cook and listening to easy music, enjoying a few minutes of peace, the sound of a car penetrated his comfortable place.

With a low growl, he opened his eyes.

Someone from his family or Gena.

He remained where he was. If his intruder was family, he'd have to force himself off the couch and make up excuses. Gena could get the kid and go.

An urgent knock rattled the wooden door. "Quinn! I know you're in there. Please open the door. I need to talk to you."

Gena. So much for solitude.

With an irritated huff, he stomped to the door and yanked it open. "What do you want?"

"Derrick."

He jerked a thumb toward the shed. "The usual."

She sagged a little, and he noticed then what he hadn't before.

"You're shaking."

"Can I come in for a minute?"

Alarmed and wishing he wasn't, he stepped aside to allow her entrance. She wore the same blue coat with rubbery Crocs, but the jaunty knit hat was missing and her blond hair was mussed.

"I was so scared."

"That I'd strangled the little twerp?"

She managed a shaky laugh. "When you aren't scowling, you're pretty funny."

He used to be Mr. Charm-and-Wit. Now he was Mr. Scowl-and-Growl.

"I'm a laugh a minute. Sit down before you collapse."

"Thank you." She slid the coat off her shoulders and folded it over the arm of his saggy couch. "Something smells amazing."

He ignored the compliment. "What's wrong?"

"I thought Derrick had run away, back to Houston."

"Wouldn't surprise me, either, but why today?"

"I found some very disturbing information on his Facebook profile." She pushed her hair back from her forehead as if needing a minute to catch her breath. "Derrick can freak me out worse than a ruptured artery."

He didn't want to know this. "So what did you find?"

"Most of his friends on there are a lot older, and they're doing things he shouldn't even know about."

He settled on the equally-saggy armchair at her elbow. "Such as?"

"Gang stuff. Guns. Drugs. I've worked in the ER enough to understand gang stuff."

TMI, his brain screamed. Too much information. He didn't want to think that the tenderhearted, hurting kid in his shed could be heading for the gutter.

"But he *didn't* run away. He's out there feeding kittens. Problem solved." *Now go away.*

"I wish. As long as he's communicating with those kids, he's in danger."

An inward sigh. She was like a tenacious linebacker.

She wouldn't quit coming at him. "So what are you going to do?"

"Ground him."

Quinn's eyes rolled up in his head. "How's that been working for you?"

"Not at all." Her lips twisted in defeat. He didn't focus there. In fact, he wasn't focusing that well at all.

"When the defense reads the play before the ball is even snapped, the quarterback better call an audible. The kid is getting away with murder, and you're sacked before you leave the pocket."

"Football analogies?" She jacked an eyebrow. "Really?"

"It's what I know. Look." He dangled his clasped hands between his knees and leaned toward her. "What you're doing doesn't work. Change strategies."

"I don't know any other strategies."

He didn't, either. Didn't want to know. Didn't want to get involved. "Let the kid come over here. Give him some responsibility. I'll see if I can talk to him."

She thought about it way too long. Her sorry opinion of him rankled.

Quinn huffed out an irritated sigh. "I promise not to hurt him."

She gave him the strangest look, like when a deer spots a human. "You have a point. He's besotted with those kittens, the first sign of caring about anything he's shown since we moved here."

"So don't give him a chance to disobey. Give him permission. Expect responsibility out of him."

The double dose of meds was affecting his judgment. He was too mellow, too accommodating. The last thing he needed was a nosy, troubled boy coming around.

Gena Satterfield looked really pretty sitting on his couch.

"Daytime maybe, but he can't come at night," she said. "He needs his sleep for school and I need mine for work."

"Do you know where he was *last* night?"

Her fingers touched her mouth. Full. Lush. Kissable. He hadn't kissed a woman in a while. New Year's Eve, maybe? He was fuzzy on that, too.

"You mean…?"

"Midnight. I drove him home."

"Why didn't I hear him? Or your truck?"

Quinn shrugged. No use going into detail. "He was here."

A frustrated groan climbed from deep in her throat. "I can save lives, but I can't control one preadolescent boy."

He wasn't about to offer comfort.

"Hey." He resisted the urge to touch her. Barely. He shouldn't have taken two pills. "You're doing the best you can in a lousy situation."

Green eyes latched on to his. "I'm scared."

Something inside him clattered around like a loose marble. Probably one of his own.

"You don't even like me."

Her face clouded. "What?"

"You don't know me, but you don't like me. Why are you dumping this on me?"

She wrestled splayed fingers through her hair, making it worse instead of better. "I don't know. The kittens, I suppose. Derrick keeps coming here and you're…here."

He chuffed a snorty laugh. "I own the place, though both of you have trouble remembering that."

"I'm sorry. You're right. I shouldn't have bothered you with Derrick's problems. I don't know why I did." She jumped up from the couch, bumping his knee, which jostled his arm and shot a flaming arrow into his elbow.

Quinn hissed through his teeth. So much for his happy hour.

Before his eyes, the worried, uncertain aunt changed into a medical professional. Like some kind of superhero spinning around in a phone booth.

The thought amused him. Super Gena. Super Nurse. She'd look good in one of those cute little superhero uniforms.

He shook his head. Too much pain medicine was playing with his faculties.

"You're still having a lot of pain? Who's your doctor? Have you seen him lately?"

"Regularly." *Whenever the pills run dry.* "I'm rehabbing again. Pain's part of the deal."

Cool, intelligent eyes assessed him. She was smart. She might figure it out. Especially if she noticed his pupils were the size of pinholes.

He shot up from the chair. "I'm making stew. Want some?"

Dumb, dumb, dumb. Now she'd be here longer.

Which didn't sound so bad, actually.

Yep. Never take two oxycodone again.

She followed him the short distance across the living room into the adjoining kitchen. "It smells amazing."

"Mama's recipe." He lifted the lid and stirred. "Looks ready."

Footsteps clattered on the porch. Quinn jerked his head toward the front door. "Might as well let him in. He knows you're here."

Derrick stomped in, shot a sullen look at Gena and slumped against the doorjamb. "Checking up on me?"

"Quinn's invited us to have stew with him. Isn't that nice?"

No, it was stupid.

"Whatever."

Really stupid.

He shot the boy an icy glare. "No one's making you eat. Go home."

"Quinn!"

"Called an audible." He turned off the stove.

"Oh." She didn't know what to say to that.

"You eating stew with your aunt and me or walking home to feed yourself? Your choice, kid." Quinn dished stew into three bowls and set them on the small table, semi-impressed that he owned three bowls, thanks to Mama and his sisters. "And don't come back with a wise answer or you're out and so are the kittens. Animal shelter."

At the last threat, Derrick's eyes widened but he dragged his feet to the table and sat.

Score one for the crippled guy.

He tossed a box of crackers on the table, added the spoons and said without apology, "No napkins. Water, milk or coffee?"

"Water is fine," Gena said. "Thank you. Show me where the glasses are and I can fill them."

He motioned toward the cabinets on either side of the sink. The kitchen boasted exactly two overhead and two lower ones. Finding a glass wasn't rocket science. Even a jock could do it.

Quinn opened the small white fridge and held up the milk. "Derrick?"

"Sure." When Quinn lifted an eyebrow, the boy mumbled, "Thanks."

While Gena ran two glasses full of water, Quinn reached for a third with his right arm. The second shelf was a stretch that tugged at the damaged biceps muscle, but he could manage.

"Let me," Gena said, bumping him to the side to get the glass.

Quinn clunked the carton onto the counter and spun to

the table. She thought he was a helpless, useless cripple who couldn't even pour a glass of milk.

He sat down and caught Derrick's stare. Was that pity in the kid's look?

"She's bossy. You have to let her do stuff." With a snicker, he muttered, "*Control* freak."

"She do that to you, too?"

"All the time."

Gena set the filled glasses in front of them. "Do what?"

The males exchanged conspiratorial glances.

"What? Are you two ganging up on me?"

Were they? "Nothing personal. My brothers and I used to do that to our sisters. Guys against the girls."

"Men got to stick together. Right, Quinn?"

Solidarity? From the rebellious, angry twerp?

"Absolutely. How's the stew?"

"Don't know. We haven't prayed." Derrick nudged his chin toward Gena. "You don't want her on you about that."

"Oh. Yeah. My bad." When was the last time he'd said grace at a meal? Maybe at the parents' house on Christmas. "Go ahead."

He bowed his head but kept one eye open to watch Gena. Her blond hair swept forward over pale, smooth cheeks as her lips moved. Not much makeup. Natural beauty.

She was a Christian like him, or like he used to be. He and God weren't exactly on the best of terms these days. He'd let God down. God had let him down. Bad deal all the way around.

"Amen."

Quinn raised his head, aware that he hadn't heard much. One more thing for God to mark against him.

Derrick hovered, elbows on the table, over the stew, alternately blowing and slurping.

"Derrick," Gena admonished.

With a sheepish grin, he said, "It's good. I'm hungry."

"Boys starve from age ten to thirty," Quinn said. "Have pity."

She reached for the cracker box. "Were you like that?"

"Buchanons are big guys. Mom says we needed a milk cow and stock in the beef and pasta industries. We were never full."

"Four of you, right?"

Four of the best men he knew. "Brady, the twins, Dawson and Sawyer, and me."

She crumbled a handful of saltines into her stew. "Three sisters, right?"

What was this? Ancestry.com? "Yeah, three. Charity, Allison and Jaylee."

"Allison was in the class ahead of me." She stirred the steaming stew round and round to cool it. "Until Dad took a job with an oil firm in Houston my freshman year."

Quinn had been a senior, wrapped up in football, recruiters and girls his age. A nerdy underclassman had not been on his Doppler.

"She was a geek," Derrick said around his spoon. "She told me so."

"A pretty one." Quinn shoved a cracker in his mouth. *Shut up, Buchanon. You're past the charmer stage.* Not that he wanted to charm Gena Satterfield. Not in his condition.

Do not take two pain pills ever again.

He swallowed the dry cracker, nearly choked and sipped the water. "Are you going to talk to Derrick about the kittens?"

Gena flashed a glance at her nephew. "I'm formulating an audible."

Derrick paused in scooping out the last bite of stew. "Huh?"

Quinn felt a smile tickle his chest but kept quiet. This was her kid to deal with, her problem.

"Derrick." She patted her mouth with her fingertips. He needed to buy some napkins. "I'm giving you permission to come here and feed the kittens."

"Yeah?" His face lit up.

She held up an index finger. "As long as you don't fall behind in school. Getting up in the middle of the night won't be easy. You can ride your bike."

Derrick shot a conspiratorial glance at Quinn. Quinn kept his expression bland. The kid didn't need to know he and Gena had already had this conversation.

"I can drive him," he said. "Pickup and delivery."

Gena's head snapped toward him. "No."

"I'm usually up anyway. Night owl."

Her lips compressed. "Oh. Right. Old habits."

"Working." And fighting the monster.

She gave a prim nod but clearly thought he was a tomcat chasing women or hanging out in clubs. As if there were clubs in Gabriel's Crossing.

"The offer's there. Take it, drive him yourself or let him walk in the dark." What did he care about this anyway?

He pushed out the chair and stalked to the stove for more stew. Derrick followed.

The woman was eating his stew but behaved as if he had leprosy. He glanced at his bent elbow. Social leprosy.

"Your offer is thoughtful but feeding the kittens and all that it entails is Derrick's responsibility."

"Then let him decide." He ladled thick, fragrant stew into Derrick's outstretched bowl.

Derrick's gaze flicked up to his. "What time? Midnight?"

"Works for me and the kittens."

"I'll meet you at the corner."

"Backyard."

"Deal."

Gena cleared her throat. Loudly. "Don't I have a say in this?"

"You called the audible. We executed it. Teamwork." Quinn tapped his elbow against Derrick's and received a smirky grin for the effort.

In spite of the annoyance swimming around behind Gena's eyes like guppies, she laughed. "All right. But if his grades go south, he's done."

Derrick flopped down at the table again. "They won't."

Feeling smugly accomplished and pleasantly attracted, Quinn set his bowl on the table. A little conversation with a pretty woman with a brain between her ears wasn't so bad. Maybe he'd invite her over again.

Scintillating conversationalist that he was, he said, "More stew?"

She pushed up from the table. "More water, thank you. Do either of you need anything else?"

Quinn arched a look at Derrick, who shook his head. "We're good."

They finished their meal, such as it was, and began clearing the table. Derrick muttered something about the kittens and slipped away.

Quinn plugged the sink and added a healthy squirt of soap. "He allergic to dishwater?"

"Probably."

"Doesn't he help you out at home?"

"Not much." She added the glasses to the filled sink. "Where are the tea towels? I'll dry."

He tossed a cloth from the drawer, pleased to have a clean one. The kid should be pulling his load. "Chores are good for him."

"He's been through so much…" She polished a glass, staring at the shine in thought. "I have trouble being tough with him because of it."

Her business. Not his. In silence, he scrubbed the bowls and handed them off to her one by one.

As she opened an upper cabinet, she paused. Her gaze swung to Quinn and back to the countertop.

"Those are really strong."

She was frowning at the prescription bottle.

His heart stopped. He should have put them away. He shouldn't have taken two. He should never have invited her to stay for dinner.

"Oh, those." He focused on washing the spoons. "Forgot they were there."

She put the towel down and picked the bottle up. "You don't take them?"

He searched for nonchalance.

"Occasionally. Docs sent them after the most recent surgery. A temporary thing while I heal. No big deal. Like I said, I forgot all about them."

He was talking too much. Lying. Hiding the truth. A little tilted on painkillers.

She let out a breath. "Good. Be careful with them, Quinn. Oxycodone can be highly addictive and hard to shake."

Right. Tell him about it.

Chapter Six

Gena heard the rumble of Quinn's truck and the quiet snick of the back door closing. She pushed aside the blankets and, in the darkness, padded in bare feet to the window in time to see red taillights disappear in the darkness.

True to his word, her gruff neighbor had arrived every night for the last week at midnight and returned around one. Derrick rode his bike to the remaining two feedings each day.

Responsibility *was* good for him, and riding a bike meant less time spent in personal contact with Quinn.

He'd said something about going out for spring football. She couldn't decide if that was a good or bad thing, considering his influence must have been Quinn.

The man was clueless about Derrick, a fact that both pleased and infuriated her, but he was no less dangerous. What if he suddenly awoke from his stupor and connected the dots?

It was a worry that nagged her day and night, especially since she didn't dislike him as much as she should.

The Quinn in the cabin by the river was different from the playboy football player who'd broken her sister's heart.

Crawling back into the warm bed, she slept until once again the truck rumbled into the back drive and Derrick returned. He amazed her, that boy she loved to distraction. She'd never expected him to hold up his end of the bargain, but he not only executed the responsibility, he hadn't grumbled about school all week.

She stopped short of crediting Quinn, though he was right about the chores. She was too soft. Maybe by summer, Derrick would be healed enough that she could be stricter.

As she snuggled into the pillow in that almost-asleep state of fog and random thoughts, the oxycodone bottle flashed by. She'd thought little of Quinn's medication since that night over stew and conversation.

Quinn Buchanon had sustained a horrendous injury. From what he'd told her, he'd suffered through multiple surgeries and reconstruction and he continued to require extensive rehab. His need for an occasional pain med was a given.

Her curious medical mind itched to examine his arm and assess the damage for herself, though he'd certainly had excellent specialists in Dallas. He favored his damaged right arm and range of motion appeared limited but he used the limb well, relatively speaking. He wasn't handicapped by the injury.

A twinge of pity stirred in her. He'd been a pro-caliber athlete with a future bright enough that the glare had blinded him to his own mortality. In his situation, the injury *would* have been a handicap.

She flopped onto her side. Quinn had lost a great deal. No wonder he was grumpy. But he was also smart and funny and kinder than he wanted her to know. Why else would he care for orphaned cats and get up at midnight for a troubled boy?

Yet he covered his tender side with gruffness and sarcasm as if he was afraid to let down his guard.

Maybe that was a good thing. A wall between them was safer for everyone.

* * *

The rain started in midafternoon and continued long after dark. They'd had a wet winter and even though March slowly released its frosty grip on North Texas, today's rain was cold.

With his sisters' goodbyes in his ears, Quinn ducked out the door of Buchanon Built and jogged to his truck before anyone could nag him about Sunday dinner at Mom's.

After stopping at the IGA for a few groceries, he drove home. Rain slashed the windows and kept his windshield wipers busy.

As he drove up to the cabin, Derrick exited the well house. Quinn almost smiled. The kittens were getting to be fat little puffs of soft down thanks to the boy's dedication.

He hopped out of the Dodge and started toward the porch. "Kittens okay?"

"Good." The boy hunched inside a plastic poncho.

Quinn paused at the door. Derrick remained in the rain as if uncertain about approaching the house. "Where's your bike?"

"Flat tire."

"You walked?"

"Sprouted wings and flew." But the wisecrack was said with a slight smile and less than the usual rancor.

"Your feathers are soaked. Come on in for a minute while I put up the groceries. I'll run you home."

This time Derrick didn't argue.

Inside the living room, he dripped on the floor. Quinn tossed him a towel. "Dry off. Your puddles, too."

Derrick shed the plastic poncho and did as he was told. "It's not this cold in Houston."

"Deal with it, Derrick. You're not in Houston. You're here."

"Not forever."

Quinn shoved the milk in the fridge and cut a glance

at the boy. Gena worried he'd run away. Would he? "The kittens need you. They wouldn't have made it otherwise."

Derrick tracked wet feet into the kitchen area and stood slouched and defeated as if his backbone wouldn't hold him upright. "I guess. They'll be able to eat by themselves soon."

Quinn shut the cabinet, glanced at the prescription bottle and quickly away. "Then what?"

"I don't know what you mean."

Are you going to run back to Houston? End up on the streets or in the gutter? Drive your aunt over the edge? "Never mind. Let's go."

On the drive to the Satterfield place, they talked about the four cats—safe ground as well as the best way to drag words out of Derrick. The boy worried over the immunity the kittens hadn't received from their mother. He discussed imprinting and socializing so the babies could become good pets. He also touted evidence that hand-raised kittens were more intelligent and affectionate. The boy was smart. Like his aunt.

Renae hadn't been a slouch in the smarts department, either. That was why he'd liked her so much. She'd matched him intellectually and could talk about something deeper than pop music and movies.

When they pulled up to the house, Quinn killed the truck and said, "Where's your bike?"

Derrick gripped the door handle. "Why?"

"I want to ride it to Houston. You can have my truck."

Derrick snickered. "I wish."

"I can fix your tire."

"Yeah? Gena doesn't know where to take it."

"My place tomorrow after you feed the cats. I'll teach you so you can do it yourself next time."

The boy contemplated the offer, his pale blue eyes more

pleased than he allowed his face to show. "Come in. You'll have to tell her. She won't believe me."

"Sure she will." But Quinn exited the truck anyway, and both males dashed through the rain to the front door.

Inside, his architect eye snapped shots of the old farmhouse, a spacious, homey place with a redbrick fireplace and shiny floors. Old-fashioned and comfy right down to a plaid sofa from decades past.

"Derrick!" Gena's voice drifted to them. "I'm in the kitchen."

Derrick hitched a shoulder toward Quinn as if to say, "Come on."

She didn't like him. She wouldn't want him barging in without warning.

He did anyway.

Gena had her back to them as she sprinkled white cheese onto a steaming casserole. Her hair was twisted up on top of her head. She wore a long red sweater over snug leggings that had him thinking about the phone-booth Super Gena again.

"Quinn's gonna fix my bike."

"You shouldn't bother him with that. I'll find a place."

"No bother," Quinn said, and was rewarded when she spun around faster than a ballerina.

"Oh. I didn't realize…"

Derrick was already across the room, scoping out the casserole. "What is that? It smells incredible."

"Lasagna. From Nana's recipe file."

"Can Quinn eat with us?"

"I'm sure he has other plans."

Right. His social calendar bulged with activity. His mouth curled. "Trying to get rid of me?"

"Don't be ridiculous."

Which wasn't an answer at all. "I'll get the bike and go."

"No. No. Derrick's right. We owe you dinner."

"It was only stew."

"Fabulous, hearty stew that saved me from cooking after a stressful…event. Stay. As soon as I set the table and toast the garlic bread, we'll eat."

"We'll take care of the table. Right, Derrick?"

"Uh, right. Sure. Plates are over here."

They worked and ate together in peace, talking about the farmhouse, the raccoons that wouldn't stay out of Gena's barn and the merits of Italian lasagna versus the Tex-Mex lasagna they were eating. Gena, he learned, was teaching herself to cook from her grandmother's recipe file.

The conversation drifted and flowed far longer than Quinn expected to remain at the Satterfield farm.

By the time they got around to clearing the table, a dull ache thrummed in his temples.

Fatigue. Long day at the office and too many interruptions at night. Maybe he needed computer glasses.

As he reached for a plate, his fingers trembled. He frowned at them. What was that all about?

He carried the stack of plates to the sink, where Gena rinsed them and loaded them into the dishwasher.

"You look a little pale," she said. "Was it my cooking?"

He glanced at the stove's digital clock. Nine. He'd skipped the six o'clock pain med because Derrick had been in the house.

Sweat prickled his neck, but he joked, "Hot salsa, I guess."

"It wasn't that hot," Derrick said. "Wimp."

"Derrick!"

Quinn appreciated the distraction. He recognized the problem, though this was the first time he'd let it go this far. Shaky. Sweaty. Achy. His body craved a pill.

He had to make a fast exit without raising suspicion.

"Seriously, Quinn. Are you all right? Is it your arm?"

He rotated his shoulder, grimacing. "Must be the rain."

Sympathetic, she said, "Want some ibuprofen?"

No, he wanted an oxy. He *craved* one. "I have some at the cabin. I should go anyway."

Her expert assessing gaze made him fidget. "If you're sure…"

Anxious now and the headache pounding harder, he handed the towel off to Derrick. "Dry, sport. I'll grab your bike and hit the road."

Derrick directed him to the bike. Trembling now, he loaded it in the back of his truck, made some comment about the midnight feeding and departed.

In less than five minutes, Quinn hit the unlocked door with the heel of his hand and headed straight for the sink and the pain reliever. His hands shook so that he battled with the childproof lid. The bottle came open with a jerk and spilled pills on the counter, into the sink and onto the floor. Quinn grabbed one and downed it, considering another.

On his hands and knees, he crawled around the kitchen floor and rescued every last tablet. They called to him. An extra pill, even two, would take the edge off faster, better.

With a guttural groan, he sat back on his heels and slapped on the lid. How had he come to this? To crawling on the floor like an animal? How had a medication that was supposed to help taken control of his life? His focus had become those times when he could legally take a pill, even to the point of setting the alarm on his watch.

He hated living like this. He had to get it under control.

No one would understand, certainly not his family. This didn't happen to a Buchanon. Mr. Football was scared and alone in his shame and pain.

"Oh, God," he heard himself say to the cold, empty kitchen.

God. Would He listen to a total mess-up like him?

Holding the bottle, he pressed his head into his hands.

His hair flopped forward but he ignored it and did something he hadn't done in a long time. He prayed.

The unexpected phone call late in the afternoon from GC Middle School put a kink in Gena's otherwise good, though busy, day at the clinic. Test results on a worried patient had come back negative for cancer. Another had sent flowers in appreciation for the care he'd received in the hospital. And she'd declared no fewer than six patients clear of last week's diagnoses. She loved when people regained health in part due to her care.

Someone buzzed her into the secure school building and she stepped into the principal's outer office, where activity hummed busier than a beehive. Students moved in and out, teachers dropped off papers or picked up others, and a secretary answered a ringing telephone every couple of minutes.

Gena glanced at her watch. She'd taken off an hour for this meeting and didn't like keeping patients waiting but Derrick came first. She prayed he wasn't in trouble…

The office door opened and a man far younger than any principal she'd ever had smiled at her. He wasn't bad looking, either. "Miss Satterfield. I'm Jackson Flint. Come on in."

Anxious and rushed, she hurried inside and took the chair he indicated directly in front of his desk. He sat down and steepled his hands, a posture that seemed synonymous with administrators.

"Is Derrick in trouble?"

"Derrick?" He frowned.

"My nephew, Derrick Satterfield."

"I know who your nephew is, but this isn't about him."

The knot between her shoulder blades eased. "I'm glad to hear that."

"Actually, I wanted to talk about you."

"Me? I'm not sure I understand."

"Dr. Ramos has served as team doctor for our football program in the past for both middle school and high school. This year he's stepping down from the middle school position and recommended you to take his place." He tilted back in his executive chair. "*Highly* recommended you. I thought he'd have mentioned it to you."

"We've been so busy at the clinic. It must have slipped his mind."

"Would you? Spring practice starts soon and we'll have some intramural scrimmages to get you acquainted. Then the fall season kicks off in August. We don't ask much. Just be there. It gives everyone peace of mind to have someone medical in the stands on game night, and in the event a serious injury occurs to one of our players, I don't have to tell you how important you would be."

The bell clock behind Mr. Flint's head indicated her time was up. She rose. "May I think about this and get back to you?"

"Comped admission to all games, high school and middle school." He smiled. "And free snacks at the concession stand."

Gena smiled, too. "You drive a hard bargain. I'll call you with my decision tomorrow after I've had time to be sure there's no conflict with my other commitments. Okay?"

He held out a hand. "I look forward to your call."

As he walked her to the door and opened it, a familiar figure slouched into the outer office followed by a redfaced woman Gena recognized as Mrs. Blassingame, the history teacher. The short squat brunette was clearly upset about something.

Gena's stomach slid south. "Derrick? What's going on?"

Eyes on the floor, her nephew jerked his shoulders

but otherwise didn't respond. Annoyance prickled under her skin.

"I'm glad you're here, Miss Satterfield," the teacher said. "Derrick is misbehaving in my class."

"What did he do?"

Mr. Flint interrupted. "Let's take this into my office."

He ushered the three of them inside. Derrick moved to the far wall and jerked his hood farther down on his forehead before shoving his hands into the hoodie pouch.

Gena glanced at the clock again. "Excuse me one moment to call my office."

Canceling an appointment at the last minute upset her. Derrick upset her.

She made the call and returned to the room where the principal was talking to Derrick. The boy was doing his best not to listen.

Gena focused on the teacher. "I need to know what exactly happened."

"That hood. I asked him not to wear it up in class. He told me to bug off."

Gena's eyes closed in frustration and embarrassment. "He said that?" She whirled on her nephew. "You said that? You disrespected a teacher?"

He sniffed and did the shoulder-roll movement that made her crazy.

"You owe Mrs. Blassingame an apology."

He didn't move.

"*Now*, Derrick."

"Derrick," Mr. Flint said in a voice that was much calmer and more rational than she felt. "Actions have consequences. An apology isn't a big thing, but it can end this conflict here and now. Otherwise…"

The silent tension in the room was worse than in a trauma-one unit. Those, she knew how to deal with.

When it became apparent Derrick was not going to

apologize, she said, "Go get your things, Derrick, and go to the car. We'll discuss this further at home."

After he slumped out of the room, she continued, "I'm sorry, Mrs. Blassingame, and I promise you, I *will* take action."

The woman's color had returned to normal. "Thank you. He's a smart boy and I realize he's grieving his mother, but oh, his attitude…"

"Trust me. I know. I appreciate your understanding."

With all the dignity she could muster and her face burning, Gena left the building.

Her good day had gone down the tubes.

Chapter Seven

"Want to have dinner with Abby and me tomorrow night? Steaks on the grill."

Quinn pushed back from his computer to eye all six feet and six inches of his oldest brother. "Do the two of you know it's March? Or does love make you immune to the chill?"

Brady grinned. "She keeps me warm, all right, but the weather's not that cold anymore, Quinn. Do you ever go outside?"

The rain had been plenty cold. "Three's a crowd."

"Not at my house, but Abby can fix you up with one of her friends. You could use a date."

"Not interested."

"What about your neighbor? The nurse practitioner."

Quinn scowled. "What about her?" Other than she occupied his thoughts almost as much as his arm and the painkillers.

"Is she dating anyone?"

"How would I know?" Was she? Nah, Derrick would have told him.

"So ask her."

"I'm busy."

Brady snorted and shook his head. "Suit yourself, but

the invitation's open. Come stag or bring a date. Just get your tail out of that cabin and stop acting like a hermit."

Easy for Brady to say. Last night, Quinn had faced the fact that he had a problem bigger than he'd realized. "I'll think about it."

Brady's giant paw squeezed Quinn's shoulder. "I'm praying for you, Quinn."

"I need it. Pray hard."

Brady gave one nod. "You got it. Love you, brother."

And before Quinn could swallow the lump in his throat, Brady moseyed out of the office.

On the way home from work, Quinn stopped to pick up a tire-repair kit. He had an air compressor and didn't need much else to fix Derrick's bike. He'd show the kid, teach him to do it the way his dad had taught him. Apparently, Derrick's dad wasn't in the picture. No dad. No mom. Lousy.

He clicked on the radio and poked the buttons until he found the Christian music station. How long since he'd listened to that?

Strangely, he felt more at peace today, as if the cathartic prayer vigil on his kitchen floor actually resolved something. It hadn't. He knew because like clockwork all day, his body had reminded him when a drug was due.

Derrick was sitting on his front porch, huddled low in his hoodie. He looked as if the world had ended.

Oh, man. A kitten must have died.

Quinn hopped out of the truck and ambled to the porch. "Hey."

"Hey."

"What's wrong?"

"Nothing."

"Kittens okay?"

"Yeah."

Quinn leaned against the porch post. "Ready to work on the bike?"

"I don't know."

He studied the dejected posture for another second, pity winning over irritation. Something was up, and the kid wanted to talk, but he didn't know where to begin.

Quinn knew how that worked. The hard words got stuffed deep until saying them was like coughing up hair balls. And who wanted to do that?

But getting them out was ultimately healing.

"Hold on a minute. I'll be right back." He went into the house, tossed the plastic sack on the table and jogged up the stairs to the loft to rummage in his closet. Finding the object he wanted, he squeezed his fingers against the laces. He could still grip a football.

He exited the house and dropped the ball in Derrick's lap. The boy looked up in surprise. "What's that for?"

"Do a guy a favor. Toss it around with me." He rotated his shoulder. "Therapy."

"For your arm?"

"And my head." *Hopefully for your head, too, you little twerp.*

"All right. Sure." Derrick pushed to a stand and executed a gentle underhand toss. A pity toss.

Sucking air through his teeth, Quinn spread the distance between them and fired the football. His elbow pulled but didn't scream. Not bad.

"You still got some heat."

Surprising, too. He hadn't thrown like that in a long time. "Sail it back to me. Show me what you got."

Derrick pulled the ball back and fired a wobbly pass. His shoulders slumped. "I stink. Coach will never let me on the field."

"I thought you didn't play anymore."

Derrick shrugged. "I changed my mind."

Quinn contemplated that piece of information and saw it as progress. If Derrick played a sport, he'd get involved with other kids. He'd learn some discipline and teamwork. "Has anyone ever showed you how to throw a spiral?"

"Like, who would do that? Gena?"

"Me." Quinn closed the gap between them and displayed the proper technique. His long, powerful fingers still did the job, still gripped the ball like a pro. "See? Ball to the chest, knees slightly bent to load the spring, feet shoulder width."

Derrick imitated the stance. "Like this?"

"Perfect. Now find your comfortable spot on the laces and draw the ball back to your ear."

Quinn took him through the steps three times, impressed when Derrick picked up the technique quickly. The kid was a good student with a natural athletic grace he apparently was unaware of. "You got it. The rest is practice."

He jogged ten yards away and held his hands in front of his chest. "Hit me in the numbers."

With each back-and-forth toss, Quinn watched the boy loosen up. Finally, he said, "Want to tell me what's bothering you?"

"Gena grounded me." Derrick torpedoed the ball with vengeance. "I'm not going back there."

Sure you are. "What happened?"

"School stinks and Gena blamed me. I'm grounded for life. She says I'm done with the kittens and she'll personally haul them to the shelter if I come here again."

No, she wouldn't. They weren't hers to haul. "She must be pretty mad."

"Steam was coming out of her ears."

"I'd like to see that."

Derrick almost smiled. "Mrs. Blassingame—she's my history teacher—hates me."

The ball sailed above Quinn's bad shoulder. Instinctively, he one-handed it. His muscles remembered. The pain was there but didn't take him to his knees. "Any idea why?"

"I told her to bug off."

"Unsportsmanlike conduct, my man. Not smart." Quinn threw the ball hard enough to make Derrick *oomph*. "I hope you had a good reason."

"I like my hood up. She hates it. Stupid rule anyway." He slapped the football back and forth against his palm. "She doesn't understand anything."

"Why is the hood so important?"

Derrick yanked the ball to his ear and threw a perfect spiral. "Kids laugh at my ear."

Now they were getting somewhere. "I don't see anything wrong with your ears."

Derrick jogged the ten yards. "See?" He tilted his head and pointed to a brown irregular birthmark along the back of one ear. "Everybody laughs 'cause it's shaped like Mickey Mouse."

"Hecklers are everywhere, Derrick. Little hearts, smaller brains. Even on the ball field."

"They made fun of you? The quarterback king?"

"Every game." Somebody wanted to challenge or intimidate the man with the golden arm. Someone wanted to prove they could take him down.

"What'd you do?"

"Outsmarted them." He'd forgotten about that. "The more they said I was too worried about my pretty face to take a tackle or that I ran like a duck or that I wasn't as good as my press, the more I studied and hit the gym to prove them wrong."

"They said that?"

"Yep."

Derrick gave him a long, appraising stare. "I don't think you're that pretty."

Quinn barked a laugh. The boy snickered, then belly-laughed. Quinn joined him, head back toward the blue sky, noticing the pleasant weather and the coming spring in a way he hadn't before. Every day wasn't rainy and cold.

He had no answers for Derrick. Not really. Feeling happy anyway, he looped his good arm over Derrick's shoulders. "Let's go fix that bicycle."

Gena didn't know whether to be touched or terrified when she followed the sound of voices around Quinn's cabin and saw the man and boy, heads together over an upturned bicycle. Her belly did a flip-flop and then tumbled all the way to the almost-green grass.

She stood at the corner of the house and watched them, aware they didn't know she was there. Quinn's manly baritone spoke softly as he guided Derrick to replace the wheel. Derrick, in deep concentration, twisted a wrench round and round while bracing the tire with one hand. Quinn pointed to something and Derrick looked up at him, completely at ease and without his usual sullen attitude.

Tenderness welled up for both of them, tenderness she didn't want to feel for Quinn Buchanon, though she had to admit the puzzling neighbor was good for her nephew. Not counting today's fiasco at school, she'd seen positive changes since the man had taken an interest.

She wasn't sure what to do about the situation. On the one hand, Quinn was good for Derrick. On the other, he was the worst possible man for her nephew to be with.

What if he tossed Derrick away like he'd done Renae? Or what if Quinn learned he was a father and wanted to take Derrick away from her?

She squeezed her eyes closed against the tender father-son scene playing out before her and sent up a plea for guidance. God had directed her here to Gabriel's Crossing for Derrick's sake and He wouldn't let either of them down now. If Derrick's camaraderie with Quinn was in His plan, though, she wished He would let her in on the outcome.

Metal clattered and propelled her into the open as Quinn flipped the bicycle upright.

"Done. Good as new." Quinn slapped the bike seat a couple of times. "Next time you'll know how to fix your own tire, but if you run into a snag, let me know."

"Thanks, Quinn." Derrick threw a leg over the bike and started to push off when he spotted Gena and stopped. "Oh."

She ambled toward him, taking her time and praying to say the right thing. He had jumped out of the SUV and run the minute they'd gotten home from school. She'd known where he was going. Exactly where she'd told him not to.

"Your tire's fixed," she said.

"Yeah." His eyes, blue like Renae's, flashed to hers and then to Quinn, who crouched over a toolbox watching them.

"Ready to go home?"

"Am I still grounded?"

She sighed. If she said yes, he might run away to Houston. If she said no, he'd never submit to her authority and could become a total disaster. Raising a child was way more complicated than she'd ever imagined.

"Audible," Quinn said, catching her eye.

"Sacked," she responded, which brought on a breath-taking smile. No wonder he'd been such a lady magnet.

"There's something extremely attractive about a woman who speaks football." His mouth clamped shut as if the statement surprised him.

She was a little shocked herself. He thought she was attractive?

Quinn pushed to a stand and tapped his toe to Derrick's bike tire. "Why don't you head home and let me talk to your aunt."

"About me?"

"Yeah, you little twerp. You." He jerked his chin in the direction of her house. "Scram."

To her total amazement, Derrick, still straddling the bike, grinned. "Midnight rendezvous and then therapy tomorrow. Right?"

"Smarter than you look. Good job." Quinn fist-bumped her nephew, and then the boy pedaled off down the road.

They were speaking some kind of male dialect she had yet to interpret, but clearly, the two had connected over something other than the kittens.

Not good. Connection could only bring heartache.

"What was that all about?" she asked.

Toting a battered red toolbox, Quinn led the way to a back door leading into the kitchen. Gena followed.

Inside, he clanged the box onto a counter and went to the sink for a long drink of water. He backhanded his moist, shiny lips, but not before she'd noticed them. Framed by a slight scruff, they were M shaped and tilted at the corners as if he smiled a lot, which he didn't. Not anymore, and she thought what a shame that was. Though stress lines bracketed his mouth in deep grooves, his was a mouth made for displaying that dynamic smile.

He reached inside a cabinet and took out a bottle of ibuprofen, shook out four and downed them.

"Headache?" Though she suspected the problem was his arm.

"Derrick and I tossed around the football. I'm out of shape."

Not from her perspective. "So that's what the therapy comment was about?"

"Yeah. I promised to give him some pointers if he'd work out my arm." The cabinet door clapped shut, but not before she saw the half-empty bottle of painkillers on the lower shelf. Frowning, she recalled the bottle had been full before, though he'd said he rarely took them.

"Why are you doing this?" she asked.

"Beats me." He led her into the living room, where they sat on the saggy couch. "He's a wad of hurt, and he kind of gets to me, I guess."

Realization clicked in Gena's head. At last she understood their connection, even if they didn't. "If anyone understands soul-deep hurt and life-changing loss, I suppose it would be you."

"Yeah. Well." He shrugged her off. "This isn't about me."

He surprised her over and over again. This man who'd run her off his land and threatened legal action was starting to look more like a big teddy bear than a grizzly.

"He got in trouble at school today. Did he tell you that?"

"Yes, and he also told me why he refused to take down the hood."

"He did?" She listened in amazement as he explained about the teasing. "He's never said a word about being bullied or teased by the other kids. Did he say who?"

"One kid mostly. Josh Miller."

"That's no excuse, though, for disrespecting the teacher."

"Agreed. He'll have to man up and pay the price for that one." He leaned toward her, his knee brushing hers so that she was acutely aware of him as a man on whom she'd once had a painful teenage crush. "Can I offer a suggestion?"

"Anything." She moved her knee an inch and then regretted it.

What was wrong with her? Was she starting to actually like Quinn Buchanon, the ogre who'd broken Renae's heart?

But he didn't seem like an ogre anymore. Like Derrick, he was hurting, and she was a trained healer.

"Consequences should mirror the crime. If an architect doesn't get the plans right, he loses jobs. If a football player goofs off on the field, he's benched. Derrick should write a letter of apology and have to do something for his teacher that shows respect. Clean chalkboards or something."

"They don't have chalkboards anymore."

He rubbed a finger over one jaw and tilted his head in a self-deprecating manner. "I'm getting old. Great wise counselor that I am."

"Don't apologize. You have a good idea." A great idea and one she should have thought of. Which showed how frazzled her brain was lately. Between Derrick's issues at school and home and her worry about her job and her unexpected neighbor, she wasn't thinking like the smart professional she was trained to be. "I'll give his teacher a call and tell her about the bullying. Then we'll figure out something he can do for her."

"Good." He sat back against the couch. "Can I ask you a question?"

Relaxed, pleased to have a solution to the Derrick dilemma, she nodded.

He gazed at her, then glanced away. She saw him swallow and wondered that the once-arrogantly confident man appeared unsure.

In a voice as soft as rainwater, he said, "What happened to Renae?"

Fear shot up her spine. He was remembering. Maybe he even suspected. "Why?"

"We dated in college. I thought you knew."

"I knew." She'd also known when Renae ran home to Houston devastated because her dream man refused to take her calls. She'd quit college and spent the rest of her life bitter and angry toward men, especially Quinn Buchanon. "She contracted bacterial meningitis a little over a year ago."

"Meningitis. That's bad news, isn't it?"

"Deadly if not treated aggressively. Apparently, she thought she had the flu, called in sick to work and stayed in bed that morning. When Derrick came home from school, she was incoherent. He called me, but by that time, she was—"

The memory of that day came back sharp as a two-edged sword. Tears clogged her throat. She cleared it. "Sorry."

His hand covered hers. "Hey. I'm sorry, too. That must have been brutal for all of you."

"Yes." The delirium, the seizures, Renae's screams and moans and pleas. The promise Gena had made to her dying sister. "For Derrick most of all."

Quinn held her hand in his. She didn't know when that had happened, but his strong, warm presence comforted her.

"There was nothing you could do."

"No. I've gone over and over that day, trying to change the outcome, trying to determine if I missed anything."

"You didn't. You're too smart."

"Thank you." She'd needed that. "I called an ambulance immediately and used every skill I possess. Nothing was enough. She…died later that night at the hospital."

They were quiet for a few minutes, each mulling the terrible loss while the refrigerator hummed and the old house creaked.

She became aware that they were alone without the buffer of a boy or a box of kittens, and Quinn Buchanon was holding her hand. He didn't seem like the enemy anymore, a truth that made her a traitor.

"I should go." Gena withdrew her hand and rose.

Quinn rose with her and before she knew what he was about to do, he stepped close and hugged her. Not a romantic embrace but a hug of compassion that wobbled her knees far worse than a come-on could have. She melted against him, clinging for a few needy minutes and basking in the scent and strength of the man she'd once dreamed about. She was still the foolish nerdy girl with a crush on her sister's boyfriend.

With great determination and more composure than she thought she could muster, Gena stepped away from his tempting comfort and walked out of his house.

Night was the worst.

Quinn flipped the remote to his satellite dish. Two-hundred-fifty channels and they all either bored him or made him mad.

He tossed the remote down and paced the thirty feet from one end of his living room–kitchen to the other.

Tonight in addition to fretting over the oxycodone that practically screamed his name, he thought about Gena.

Better her than the pills.

Hugging her was the kind of thing the old Quinn would have done. A girl needed a hug, he was happy to oblige. But Gena had bolted.

He gave a short laugh. "First time that ever happened."

He rubbed his whiskers, hearing the scratch, the only sound in the cabin besides the screaming in his head. His heart was starting to beat erratically. He could feel it in his neck. Soon he'd feel the thud in his chest and temples and then the headache would start.

He glanced at the clock. If he could go ten more minutes, he'd be an hour past his scheduled pill, a small victory but still a win.

Maybe he should call Gena, apologize for stepping out of bounds, however unintentionally.

"Where's the stupid phone?" A rummage under papers, a stack of clothes on the bed and the sofa cushions turned up nothing.

"When was the last time…" He knew then and dug the device from the jacket he'd worn to a job site on Monday. Three days ago.

After another search for the charger, he plugged in and sank onto the bed. Her number remained in his log and he dialed.

Gena answered on the second ring. "Gena Satterfield."

"Very professional."

A pause came over the line before, "Who is this?"

Ah, yes, he still left an impression. "Quinn."

"I thought so." The answer made him feel a little better.

"Do I owe you an apology?"

She didn't pretend to misunderstand. "No."

"If I overstepped or offended you, I didn't mean to. I intended…" What had he intended? To enjoy the feel of her body close to his? To lock her unique scent into his memory?

"Don't think anything more about it. It was only a hug."

No, it wasn't. "Right. Okay. How did things go with the twerp?" Safe ground.

"If you mean did Derrick bolt for Houston, the answer is no. He was surprisingly mellow and agreeable when I talked to him about consequences."

"Good to hear."

"Whatever you said to him, thank you."

"All I did was fix his tire." Quinn refused to take credit. He was no one's role model. He couldn't even handle his own life, much less some snot-nosed kid's.

He shifted positions to cradle the phone between his shoulder and ear while staring at the empty walls of his bedroom. No pictures. No posters. No awards. They were all packed away somewhere in a storage building.

Before he could consider the reasons not to, he blurted, "My brother's grilling steaks tomorrow night with his fiancée, Abby."

A smile lilted from her voice. "I know Abby. I really like her, and her little girl is precious."

"Good. He invited us."

"Us?"

That hadn't come out right. "Me, and he said I could bring a…someone. He suggested you."

"Me? Oh, I don't know…"

He was more disappointed than he wanted to be. "I understand. No big deal."

"I haven't said no, Quinn." Her tone was gentle, as if she knew what he was feeling. "What about Derrick?"

"Bring him."

"Steaks, you say?"

A smile curled in his chest and almost made it to his mouth. "Brady's an expert on the grill and Abby can cook anything. You'll love his house. He built it himself."

"Tempting, but—"

"It's only a meal, Gena. You have to eat."

He held his breath while the line hummed and she considered. He'd been shot down very few times in his life. Ignored, yes, but outright refused, not many. But he hadn't tried in a long, long time. Was he ready to stick his neck out this way?

"Okay, then. What time?"

His shoulders relaxed. "Is six forty-five too early? I'll pick you up."

"Six forty-five is perfect. That gives me time to come home and shower off the disinfectant."

They talked a few more minutes, mostly about nothing, before ending the call. He glanced at the phone's digital clock. He'd made it, thanks to Gena. Though his head throbbed and his pulse rattled in his throat, the oxy hadn't won this round.

He lay with the phone pressed to his chest, mulling the call. He'd made a date. With a medical professional.

Sure, he was attracted to her, but the timing couldn't be worse.

He rolled off the bed and headed for the kitchen cabinet.

Chapter Eight

She shouldn't have. She knew better, knew she was court-
ing trouble, but Gena had said yes.

At the moment, she didn't regret the decision. Since
moving to Gabriel's Crossing, she'd been so busy with her
medical practice she'd had minimal time for a social life.
She wanted that to change. Soon. Plus, she liked Abby
Webster and wanted to know the Buchanon family better.
Tonight was the perfect opportunity.

Reasonable or foolish, those were her rationalizations
for accepting Quinn's invitation.

"Your house is fabulous, Brady," she said to Quinn's
tall, rust-haired brother, who, along with Abby, had given
her the grand tour of the native rock-and-golden-wood
structure.

"It's big like Bwady." Abby's daughter, five-year-old
Lila, turned her pert little face and spoke as she pushed
her walker along in front of the group. The pretty child
had spina bifida but neither she nor her mother allowed
the challenges to slow her down. She was a sunny, lively
youngster who tugged at Gena's heartstrings. Someday
she wanted a little girl to love.

"Watch out, squirt." Derrick hovered along beside Lila
like a mother hen. "Door facing."

Lila giggled. "I know."

Of course she did. Brady's home was roomy and accessible and allowed the child plenty of freedom. She probably knew every bump and danger from experience.

"Brady," Abby said. "The steaks?"

"Oops. Better check them." He kissed Abby on the forehead and lingered, his eyes on hers, as though five minutes apart was half a lifetime. Mushy, but sweet and affirming to know that love could happen.

She glanced at Quinn, who watched Derrick and Lila with interest. Her pulse ticked up, and thoughts of love were replaced by fear that Quinn would see what he shouldn't.

As a distraction, she said, "Let's go out on the patio, too. The weather is great today."

Quinn came alongside her. "Spring will sneak up on us soon."

"Judging by today, it already has."

"Pseudo spring. We'll get some more windy, chilly days."

"This is my favorite time of year. Jacket and sweater weather when green grass pushes up between the brown blades. Spring is so…hopeful."

"I could use some of that," he said, and she wondered if he meant spring or hope.

They crossed the enormous open living/dining room to the French patio doors. Gena was careful not to walk too close to him, because each time she did, Quinn placed his hand against her back and sent her thoughts in dangerous directions.

Abby stopped in the kitchen to check something that smelled delicious. Lila chattered at Derrick, showing him the big-screen TV and introducing him to Dawg, Brady's large, affable brindle canine.

Her nephew, rubbing the dog's ears, surprised her by asking the little girl, "Want to watch cartoons?"

Lila's walker clattered to a halt. "Do you?"

Judging by the eager expression, Lila loved the idea.

"Sure. Come on. Show me your favorite."

Cartoons? For Mr. Too-Cool-for-Kids'-Stuff-Anymore?

Gena exchanged glances with Quinn. In an undertone, she muttered, "Who *is* he?"

"Lila's got a way about her, and she has Dawg."

"Do you think Abby will let me borrow them? For about six years?"

Quinn chuckled and pushed open the door, letting her walk through first. Again, he touched her back, lightly with the tips of his fingers, but she felt the warmth all the way to her heart. He'd been the perfect gentleman tonight, friendly and pleasant. On the way over, they'd talked about her medical practice and she'd shared some of her more difficult cases, without names or breaking ethics. She was a stickler for ethics. Quinn had asked astute questions and made smart comments as if he didn't mind her geeky intellect. He was, she realized, a pretty smart guy himself.

It suddenly occurred to her to ask, "Did you design this house?"

"Brady and I together. He knew what he wanted. Being the architect, I drew up the plans and blueprints."

"Now I understand the success of Buchanon Built Construction. You're very good."

He looked uncomfortable. "Ah, well…it's only a job. Not like what you do."

"You're too modest." She never expected to say *that* about Quinn Buchanon. "Shelter is a basic need, but a beautiful, well-built home is something special."

He motioned to a patio chair, clearly wanting to change the subject. "Sit?"

She nodded.

Did he think his work was less important somehow? Or was he resentful because he'd rather play football?

The tantalizing smell of meat smoke drifted on the cool evening air from a large, stainless grill, though Brady dwarfed it. He shut the lid with a clang.

"Won't be long. You two want a Coke or some tea?"

"I can get it," Quinn said. "You hang with those steaks."

"Let me." Gena rose. "I should see if Abby needs any help anyway."

"Anytime I can get a woman to wait on me," Brady said, "I'm smart enough to say yes."

Gena laughed. "Don't get used to it. What will you have?"

Quinn settled back. "Sweet tea."

"Same here." Brady pointed a barbecue fork at her. "And don't preach healthy nutrition to us."

Lifting her hands, she smiled. "I'm off duty."

She slipped inside the house, where Lila's infectious giggle rivaled the *Tom and Jerry* music. Derrick, sweetly attentive to the special-needs child, sprawled on the floor with the dog and pretended to enjoy the cartoon. Quinn was right. Lila possessed a gift with people.

"What can I do to help?" she said to Abby, who moved around the kitchen with the confident proficiency of someone who worked in food service, which she did. Even though she was engaged to one of the Buchanons, who weren't exactly poor, she continued to wait tables at The Buttered Biscuit Café. Gena found that admirable. Women, she believed, should be able to stand on their own two feet, no man required. Though lately, she thought having a man around could be…enjoyable.

"Most everything is ready, but you could get the condiments from the fridge while I finish up this salad."

"And drinks. I have orders for two sweet teas without a health lecture."

"That's the Buchanon boys." Abby smiled, shredding lettuce into a clear bowl as she talked. "My Brady loves his sweet tea."

"Sweet tea and you."

Abby rested the knife against the bowl. "It's crazy how much we love each other. Sometimes I still can't believe how blessed I am to have met that big, gorgeous hunk of Buchanon." Her face went dreamy. "And he loves Lila, too, as if she was his own. I am humbled by having so much love in my life."

At the light in Abby's eyes, Gena refused to be envious, but oh, how wonderful to have found your true love. Even as a busy, fulfilled career woman, she'd never planned to face life alone. Yet here she was, past thirty and still waiting for Mr. Right. "You're all very fortunate."

"We know and we're careful not to take each other for granted." She placed a tomato on the cutting board and gave it a whack. "What about you and Quinn? Are you seeing a lot of each other?"

The question gave Gena pause. "If you mean dating, no."

"That surprises me." Abby's brow buckled. "You're the first woman Quinn's ever brought here, and Brady says he talks about you at work, something he *never* does. I naturally thought…"

Gena's heart dipped. He talked about her? She wanted to ask what he said but thought she might be better off not knowing.

"We're neighbors, and Quinn has these kittens Derrick is enamored of."

Abby whacked the tomato a few more times. "Whatever the reason, we're thrilled he invited you tonight. Brady worries about him, prays for him, nags him. Most times when he invites him over, Quinn won't come at all."

"Why not?"

"I wasn't around when the accident happened, but according to Brady, Quinn has never been the same. The Buchanons are very close, but Quinn moved to Dallas for a long time after the accident and seldom came home. At first he used the doctors and hospitals as an excuse and then he went to work for a large architectural firm. They feared he'd never come home again."

The exact reason Gena hadn't worried about encountering him when she moved here. She'd heard he lived in Dallas. "He told me he's only been back in Gabriel's Crossing a couple of years."

"Yes. Living in that old cabin like a reclusive hermit. Rarely socializing. Grumpy and silent and alone. He used to be a woman magnet but now he never dates. Brady thinks he hasn't dealt with the anger even though he claims he has."

"Terrible, what happened to him."

"I guess he was really something."

"He still is."

Abby tilted her head, dark eyebrows raised. "I thought you were only neighbors."

"We are." But she couldn't help recalling the warmth of his hug or the kindness he'd shown Derrick, or worse, the painful torch she'd carried for him in high school. "What I meant was he's a gifted architect. Why isn't that enough?"

"It is, but he's the one who needs to believe it," Abby said. "If you'll take those drinks and condiments out to the table, I'll roust Derrick away from Lila and we'll bring the rest."

Gena loaded a tray and carried it to the patio, pondering the conversation with Abby. She worried about Quinn, too, though at first her concerns had been for Derrick and the promise she'd made to Renae. Now she worried about the man himself and about her growing feelings for him.

He was cocked back in the padded lounger, sunglasses

on top of his golden head, eyes narrowed in focus some-where far off into the deep cedar-and-oak woods that bor-dered the expansive back lawn. His hand rested on his bad shoulder.

She set the tray on the table next to him. "Are you in pain?"

He turned his focus to her. She suffered a momentary thrill at having those hazel eyes on hers.

"Not bad."

"Anything I can do?"

"You're off duty, remember?"

Her words came back to bite her. "Friends help friends."

His lips curved the slightest amount. "Are we friends?"

The question troubled her. Were they? Could she allow them to be? But she liked him. Maybe she more than liked him.

"I'm a healer. Seeing someone in pain bothers me." *You bother me.*

"The pain comes and goes. I'm okay."

"Damaged nerves?"

"Yeah. The docs are working on that."

"Nerve pain is the worst."

"It's better since the last surgery."

She handed him the glass of iced tea. Their fingers brushed in the exchange and pleasure shot through her arm. Pleasure, not pain such as he lived with every sin-gle day.

Quinn had suffered a long time from the hunting acci-dent that had taken so much from him. Pity welled in her and behind it came another, stronger emotion. Touching him and being touched did that to her. Like the night he'd hugged her. Putting his arms around her meant nothing to him. He'd said as much. But that moment meant some-thing to her.

She spotted Abby through the glass with her hands full

and hurried to open the door. Sitting next to Quinn gave her crazy thoughts and feelings. All things considered, she had to get herself under control.

Quinn followed Gena a with narrowed gaze, then carried his tea glass to the grill to stand next to his brother.

"I like her," Brady said. "I'm glad you brought her along."

"She's all right."

"I got eyes. You like her, too."

Quinn shoved the fingers of his good hand in his back jeans pockets and scowled. "You're in love, an emotion that addles the brain cells. You see everything through the love filter."

Brotherly blue eyes that always saw too much studied him until he glanced away. "Are you saying you *don't* like her?"

He wasn't saying anything. Not another word. He handed his brother a serving platter. "Steak is done enough."

"We're talking about Gena, not steak. You like her or she wouldn't be here." He plopped the juicy beef onto the platter. "Her kid's not bad, either. Lila and Dawg approve."

"Derrick's a little twerp, but he kind of gets under your skin. We've tossed the ball around a few times."

"He plays football?"

"He does now." Come to think of it, the twerp had taken a new interest in the game after the pair of them started working out each evening.

"Thanks to you," Gena said, coming up beside him.

How long had she been there? Had she heard the conversation? But then again, what did it matter if she overheard? No matter how much he liked her, Quinn knew the score. Gena was a ten and Quinn a zero.

"His coach says he has potential," she said.

"He does. He has the size, too, or he will have from the looks of him, but he doesn't know the fundamentals."

"The team is overloaded with kids," she said. "I doubt the coach has much time to work with them one-on-one."

"Quinn can teach him." This from his mouthy brother. "If anyone knows the game inside and out, it's Quinn."

Quinn stiffened. "Water under the bridge."

Gena touched his good arm. "You've been great for him."

Yeah, that was him, he thought caustically. Great with kids. Great with people. Great at running his own life. He was great all over the place. "I taught him a spiral. Anyone could do that."

"Not true." Brady set the steak platter on the glass patio table. "You know, I have this idea." He flashed a grin. "One of my undeniably brilliant thoughts. You should drop by practice and show the kids some pointers."

Gena got a funny look on her face. A crease appeared between her eyebrows.

What was that all about? She didn't want him at Derrick's practice now that she was the new team doc. Maybe she was afraid he'd embarrass her or the kid? Or maybe she thought he'd embarrass himself?

He probably would.

"Think about it, Quinn," Brady said. "You have skills even the coach can't emulate."

Used to have skills. He was done. He rubbed at his shoulder, the constant reminder of who he no longer was.

To his relief, the rest of the dinner party exited the house. Maybe now Brady would stop talking about the impossible.

"What do you think, Derrick?" his nosy brother asked.

"About what?" The boy slid the salad bowl onto the table, gaze cautiously moving from adult to adult. "Am I in trouble?"

"Nah, I was telling Quinn he ought to stop by your football practice sometime."

Derrick flashed a look at Quinn. "Really? You'd do that?"

Quinn shifted uncomfortably. Why couldn't his brother shut up?

"Quinn's a busy man," Gena interrupted, still wearing that frown in the middle of her forehead.

Derrick's shoulders slumped but he pulled off the cocky "don't care" attitude. "Go figure. Big man on campus is too busy for the lowly scrubs."

Quinn wasn't sure if he was grateful for the reprieve or resentful of Gena's attitude. He glared at her, torn between rescuing the kid or himself.

In the end, he squeezed the top of Derrick's shoulder. "I'll think about it. Okay?"

There. A noncomment gave him an out without destroying Derrick. Subject closed.

Escaping the miserable conversation and Derrick's accusing stare, Quinn stooped to help Lila into a booster chair. He could still lift a five-year-old.

Her baby teeth gleamed, melting him. Like the rest of the Buchanons, he'd walk through fire for this tiny bit of humanity. Brady practically had.

"Thank you, Uncle Quinn."

"He's not your uncle yet, Lila," Abby said.

"I'm pwacticing."

"Call me 'Uncle' anytime, Miss Lila. I like it."

She clapped her small hands. "See, Mommy? He's so nice. Like Bwady."

Him? Nice? The kid saw the world through rose-colored glasses. If she only knew where he'd been and what he'd been through—

His thoughts skidded to a halt. Lila did know. She understood chronic pain and ongoing medical treatments. She understood a condition that would never go away.

And yet she glowed. She smiled. She loved. She embraced every day as a blessing.

Quinn got a really strange feeling in his gut that had nothing to do with pills, pain or the succulent steaks waiting on the table.

A man could take a lesson from Lila Webster.

By the time the evening rolled to an end, the patio was cleared, and several hours of good company and conversation had passed, Quinn's mind had started to wander. He'd popped four ibuprofen in Brady's kitchen, which had helped, but now the crawly feeling was coming on hard and fast. He wasn't in pain from the arm. He was in pain for a pill.

He checked his watch. Past time. He didn't want to get shaky and weird on Gena the way he had before.

Faking a yawn, he stretched his arms as high over his head as possible. "This has been great, Abby. Brady. But I think we should call it a night."

"I'm thrilled you came." Abby followed him into the kitchen, where he put his dishes in the sink. "Having you here means a lot to your brother."

The two of them were alone except for the children in the living room. Derrick, the night's surprise, read a picture book to an enchanted Lila. That kid had potential.

"Brady misses you, Quinn."

Quinn dragged his attention back to Brady's fiancée. "He has you."

"You know how he is about family. He's the fixer, the patriarch of sorts. He worries about you. They all do."

The last thing he needed to hear. "Nothing to worry about. Tell him I said that."

"Tell him yourself. Better yet, prove it." She put a hand on his elbow. "We're praying for you."

To his relief, Brady and Gena came inside with the remaining dishes and leftovers and the conversation ended. He needed to get home. He should have brought an oxy with him, but he didn't want to chance Gena seeing it. After all, he'd said he rarely took them.

But he was long overdue. He'd been trying harder, spacing them out further and further past the usual four-hour period. He'd not taken a dose for over six hours.

He grabbed his jacket from the back of the couch and said to Gena, "Ready?"

At her strange, questioning look, Quinn realized he'd been abrupt.

"You have work tomorrow." That should clear up his meaning. He was getting jittery. "Derrick, ready?"

The boy and his five-year-old adorer looked up. "Can I finish reading this book to Lila?"

"Pwease, Uncle Quinn."

Instead of the refusal on his tongue, he said, "Okay. Make it fast," and slid onto one of Brady's bar stools to make small talk with the adults. As soon as Derrick closed the book, he stood. "Thanks for dinner."

"Our pleasure," Brady said. "Let's do it again Sunday after church at Mom's."

"I'll think about it." He was surprised to actually mean it. He'd enjoyed tonight until the drug started calling his name.

Abby stood beside his brother, beaming earnestly. "Bring Gena and Derrick." She turned to Gena. "You will come, won't you? The Buchanon bunch is such great fun and Sundays after church are the best. Karen cooks like a pro, everyone brings a dish or snack, and we visit and relax. Lots of laughter."

Gena flashed a look at him. "I'll think about it, too.

Thank you for the invitation and the incredible steak. Your home is gorgeous."

"Brady's home," she corrected.

"Yours, too, as soon as I can get a ring on your finger." Brady snugged Abby close to his side and kissed her nose. "Want to get married tomorrow?"

Abby laughed, but Quinn saw no humor. Cut the chit-chat. He needed out…of…here.

Sweat popped out on the back of his neck, and he was never as relieved as when they'd finally ended the world's longest goodbyes and headed home in his truck.

In the dim confines of the pickup cab, Derrick leaned over the seat. "You gonna come to my practice?"

The last thing he wanted to talk about right now.

Scowling at the dark road ahead, he said, "No one wants a has-been with a crippled arm."

Certainly not one who might be addicted to painkillers.

"The guys got all slobbery when I told them you taught me that spiral. Like you're some kind of legend or something."

"You see?" Gena's pale face appeared almost luminescent in the dash lights. Soft and touchable. "The only person dwelling on your disability is you."

"Yeah? Based on what scientific data? A couple of misguided middle schoolers?" When did she jump on the bandwagon? An hour ago, she'd frowned as if he was Hannibal Lecter.

"You throw the ball with Derrick, you work on your cabin and your truck and your family's projects. You do anything you want to do except play pro ball. I think your biggest problem is between your ears."

He grunted but the accusation took root.

Befuddled, both by the desire for oxy and the realization that he might be the cause of his own misery, Quinn looked for a way out of this conversation.

Derrick rescued him. "You don't have to. It's no big deal." Which meant it was.

With a sigh of guilt, he turned his head toward the boy and pity bloomed. The kid had a boatload of hurt. Why make it worse? "I'll stop by practice sometime. Okay?"

"Yeah?"

"Yeah. Now put your seat belt on."

"Whatever." But he sat back and the seat belt clicked.

At the Satterfield farm, Quinn pulled into the drive and stopped in front of the house. Derrick hopped out and loped inside. Gena didn't move.

His head pounded and his insides had begun to tremble. Slightly, but enough to feel as if the flu was coming on. The pills, the stress, the arm pain—a set of unwanted triplets bearing down on him.

A couple more minutes was all he needed. Get Gena out of the truck and to the door and make his escape. He reached for the door handle. His fingers quivered, so he snatched them back.

"Quinn?"

"Yeah?"

"What's wrong?"

"Not a thing. I'll walk you to the door."

"Don't lie to a CRNP. You're perspiring and a little shaky. If I took your pulse, I'm guessing it would be rapid and thready."

"Tired. That's all. And the arm. You know." He had to get out of here.

"I don't believe you."

He squeezed his eyes shut. The hammer in his head pounded them open. "I'm okay, Gena. A little nauseated. Must have been the salad dressing."

He reached for the door again, but a hand on his arm stopped him. "Could I ask you something?"

No! "Sure."

Be calm. Just remain calm.

"This has happened twice that I know about." Her experienced fingers slid down his arm to his wrist. "Your pulse is galloping. You're sick."

"Maybe I am. The flu. I should get home."

"How long have you been taking oxycodone, Quinn?" Her voice was soft and understanding, if annoyingly persistent. It was all he could do not to blurt the ugly truth.

"Not long." He lied.

Her silence lingered until he knew she didn't believe him.

"If you need help…"

"No."

"I can help you get off them. I've done it before."

"You saw me take those ibuprofen. They probably upset my stomach."

"I thought the culprit was salad dressing," she said, gently.

"Whatever." Sounding too much like the twerp, he reached for the door handle and this time, he got it open. Fighting to appear normal, he rounded the truck and opened her door.

They walked in silence to her front porch. A yellow light glowed from somewhere inside the house. In the shadows, he felt safer, as if the darkness could hide him as well as his personal darkness.

"Thanks for coming with me," he managed to say.

"Quinn—"

He put a finger over her lips. No more talk of his struggle with pills. But her lips felt so soft against his skin, he lingered there and found her gaze in the dimness.

Her fingers circled his and slowly tugged away his hand. "I meant what I said. I'm here if you need help—"

He knew no other way to shut her up, so he leaned in close and kissed her.

The desire for a painkiller retreated to the back of his mind. He forgot about his damaged body, about the pills, about everything except the woman in his arms. He stepped nearer, slid both arms around her and tugged her up to him. He was far taller, but she fit. Nicely.

He explored a bit, remembering how much he enjoyed kissing a woman he cared about. She made a small noise of surprise but didn't pull away, as if she, too, had been wondering about this moment.

He snagged on the thought. *Had* he been wondering?

Yes. Oh, yes.

Gena Satterfield. Smart. Beautiful. A people-loving Christian who would fit perfectly with the Buchanon clan.

Whoa. He broke the kiss and stepped away. A Christian woman would want nothing to do with him, not like this. "I should go."

Her hand was on her mouth, her eyes wide. "Yes."

He trembled all the more, from her closeness, from the need for pain relief and from the desire to hold her again.

Without another word, but with his mind reeling and his body screaming, he trotted across the yard to his truck and drove away.

Chapter Nine

Gena lay awake in the darkness. The old farmhouse creaked and settled in familiar, comforting groans that usually lulled her to sleep. A tree branch rested shadow fingers on the foot of her bed, comforting as well because she and Renae had climbed that tree, played beneath its shade and snacked on its green apples.

She usually slept like a baby in the bosom of good childhood memories, but tonight Quinn's kiss kept her wide-awake. She wasn't a complete fool. He'd kissed her to shut her up, but something had happened between them. He'd felt it, too, and was as shell-shocked as she was. Tenderness. Caring. Passion.

A teenage infatuation was one thing, but she was in danger of falling in love with a man who apparently had a drug problem. A man she'd promised to despise all the days of her life.

If that wasn't enough to keep her awake and praying for direction, she allowed Derrick to hang out with him, to form a bond, to grow attached. Before bedtime he'd admitted that Josh Miller didn't tease him anymore, because he knew Quinn.

With a frustrated moan, she tossed onto her back and stared at the moonlight-dappled ceiling. "What should I do, Lord? Show me what's best for Derrick and how to juggle my promise to Renae with this sweet joy growing in my heart. Show me how to help Quinn, because if I'm right, he's in trouble."

Her brain took over again and she stopped praying. Wouldn't it be safer to stay away from Quinn altogether? But Derrick wouldn't and she didn't want to.

All her life, Gena had been the geeky sister in the shadow of the ultra popular Renae, a girl who'd broken hearts all over Texas. Until Quinn had broken hers.

Heartbreaker. Player. User. Those were some of the milder words Renae had called Quinn. Was he really that heartless? Was she a complete idiot, after what her sister had endured, to still yearn for the former gridiron star?

Groaning again, she clenched the sheet with both fists. For someone with a high IQ, she felt really dumb tonight. This was a problem she couldn't solve with logic and rational thought. The heart, she realized, was never rational.

The rumble of an engine broke the quiet country night. Quinn was here for Derrick. Her irrational heart threatened to push her out the door and into that big ole truck with him.

She listened as the back door squeaked open and in less than a minute, the truck rumbled away so two troubled males could care for a batch of orphaned kittens. She should worry about her nephew, but she couldn't. In his gruff, manly way Quinn was fond of Derrick. He wouldn't hurt him, not intentionally.

There was the problem. Hurt was hurt whether intentional or not, and Quinn had the power to devastate an eleven-year-old boy.

She'd made a promise to her dying sister, and every single time Derrick was with Quinn, the promise was in danger of being broken.

If he learned the truth, what then? Could she ever forgive herself for betraying Renae? The adoring young woman Quinn had abandoned when she needed him most?

A man like that didn't deserve to know his son. *Undeserving jerk* was the mantra she and her parents lived by.

But was Quinn still that man?

Maybe. Maybe not, but if he was dependent on painkillers...

Frustrated, uncertain and torn between a promise to her sister and her feelings for Quinn, Gena gave up sleep and flipped on the bedside lamp. She would read her Bible until Derrick returned and pray some more for an answer to the impossible.

Long after they'd fed the kittens and he'd returned Derrick to the farmhouse, Quinn lay awake in his cabin, thinking, not because of the pain or even the desire for another pain tablet. Sleep wouldn't come because of Gena.

He hadn't meant to kiss her but now that he had, he had to face the facts. Way beyond the attraction stage, something powerful pushed against his rib cage, taking root, winding around his heart like a perfumed vine. He hadn't been in this spot in years. Not since Renae had twisted him into a thousand different knots and left him to suffer alone.

Renae. Gena. Something in him gravitated toward the Satterfield girls.

Oddly, Gena bore little resemblance to Renae, neither in looks nor in personality. Renae had run him in circles, but the serious sister surprised him, disturbed him and, yes, even soothed him. He admired Gena. *Admired*, a word he had never before used in conjunction with a woman he wanted. Pretty shallow of him, now that he thought about it. Gena was not only smart, she wasn't afraid to nail him when he was wrong. And the way she'd felt in his arms was stunning, powerful, indescribable. She fascinated him.

His family had tiptoed around his cranky, unpredictable moods. They pitied him. Not Gena. She told him to get over himself. Yeah. She scared him to death.

As he'd feared would happen, that brain of hers saw what others didn't. She recognized the symptoms of oxycodone dependency, although tonight he thought he'd done an adequate job of covering and denial.

He could never admit she was right. Never. A man had pride. If he confirmed her suspicions, he could throw any hope of a romance with her down the toilet.

He hadn't allowed himself a real relationship in years. He dated occasionally. But a true give-and-take relationship hadn't appeared on his agenda since before the accident. Since Renae.

Did he dare take the chance? Or would Gena see him as her cranky neighbor who might be a medical case? A patient she could help? A crippled loser dependent on a painkiller to get him through the night?

Quinn stacked his good arm behind his head and sighed.

Better keep his hands and lips and aberrant thoughts to himself until he had the drug under control. If he could.

Thanks to her accusation that his disability was in his head, he'd fought the monster until nearly midnight, skipping not one but two doses of his frenemy. He was almost proud of himself.

He used to be a winner.

Maybe he could be again.

Gena stood, cross armed, on the sidelines of the GC Middle School football field, huddled inside her Windbreaker. Spring practice had begun and forty-plus players roamed around in black helmets with yellow flags sticking out of their back pockets. No hitting, tackling or physical contact yet, thank goodness.

"Hey, Doc." A thirty-something coach jogged in her direction, his Tigers warm-up jacket flapping open to reveal a trim, muscular physique. He would have to be in shape to keep up with all the energy on this field.

"Technically, I'm a nurse," she corrected with a smile when he reached her side.

"*Nurse Practitioner* is too hard to say in a hurry. Doc will do." When he grinned, laugh lines appeared around deep-set eyes. He wasn't bad looking but he didn't compare to Quinn, at least not in her view. "The principal said you might help us out with the middle school team."

She had to get Quinn out of her head today. "Would that work for you? Me being a female?"

"Absolutely. You've already gained a strong reputation around town. Half these boys claim you as their doctor already."

She'd recognized and spoken to several.

"Nurse," she said again. "But if that's too complex, try Gena."

"Grant Richardson, head coach." He aimed a referee's whistle toward the field. "Harris. Jenson. You boys quit horsing around. Five wind sprints."

Groans erupted, but the culprits exchanged glances and then took off down the field to the razzing laughter of their teammates.

"Spring practice is mostly about conditioning and fundamentals, but we'll have five scrimmages," the coach said. "Can you be here for those?"

"Mr. Flint gave me the schedule. With Derrick playing, I'd planned to attend most games anyway." She shaded her eyes against the sun. If Derrick had seen her, he was pretending not to. "How's he doing?"

"Surprisingly well. I see improvement at every practice. All of a sudden, he's gone from bad attitude to gung ho."

Thanks to Quinn.

"Our neighbor has been showing him some things."

"Quinn Buchanon?" He nodded. "Derrick told some of the other boys. They're impressed."

"Do you know Quinn?"

"Used to. He was a rock star in this town. Best football player I ever saw." He crooked a finger at one of the players, who started jogging toward the sidelines. "I gotta get back to it. Stick around and watch as long as you like. And thanks. Glad to have you on board."

He jogged out onto the field to meet the player. Gena folded her arms again against the chill, glad she'd tossed the jacket over her scrubs. She had some time today, her afternoon off from the clinic, though she was on call for emergencies. She could watch for a while.

As a teen, she'd had her head stuck in a book most of the time, but she'd never missed a football game, especially after she discovered the Mighty Quinn.

As she watched her nephew lope around the field, an unsettling déjà vu came over her. With his long, lanky body, the arm cocked back to throw and the helmet in place, Derrick resembled his athletic father.

She'd never thought they looked alike before. Derrick was Renae's son all the way. Until now.

Her troubled gaze was glued to Derrick when she heard someone approach. Turning slightly, her heart lurched.

What was he doing here?

Hands deep in the pockets of an olive-green jacket, Quinn said, "Mad at me?"

"Should I be?"

Eyes cool, his face shrugged as if her answer didn't matter. "Your call."

Pulse pounding, she shifted her gaze away from him. If he wanted cool, she could do that. "I don't have time for anger."

He released a long, slow breath as if her reply relieved

him and shifted, the material of his jacket swishing. "Do you have time for dinner on Sunday?"

Her gaze swung back to him. In the sunlit afternoon with only a few clouds skittering past, the tips of his hair gleamed golden and the grooves around his mouth deepened. She'd kissed that mouth and liked it. Too much. A Judas kiss to her sister's memory.

"If you're asking me to dinner as an apology for kissing me, then the answer is no."

His gaze fell to her mouth. "I won't apologize for that. I'm not sorry."

Ker-thump.

"Neither am I." Confused and conflicted, but not sorry. She'd always wondered what kissing Quinn would be like, and the reality outdistanced her imagination by a mile. "Quinn, about the other night. Are you ok—?"

He cut her off. "Is the little twerp out there?"

"Number sixteen."

His head tilted. "Sixteen?"

"Is that important?"

"Sixteen was my number."

Oh, boy. Derrick must have known.

About that time, Derrick spotted her, or maybe he saw Quinn, because he broke from the group and trotted to the sidelines. In the helmet, his head looked too big for his body. A mouth guard dangled from his grill.

When he pulled off the helmet, sweat plastered his hair against his forehead.

"Did you see that pass I threw? Twenty yards to the sweet spot."

She hadn't, but his face was so openly eager she couldn't disappoint him. "Awesome. Coach says you're doing great."

"Yeah." He shifted onto one cleat, attention on the big man at her side. "I didn't think you'd come."

Quinn almost smiled. "Surprise."

It certainly was. Heart-attack surprise.

Gena's cell phone vibrated against her side. She read the text and said, "I'm on call. I have to go. Emergency. See you at home, okay?"

Derrick's shoulder twitched. "I guess."

His reply wasn't exactly respectful but it was an improvement over "whatever."

Gena had taken a half-dozen steps toward her Xterra when Quinn's voice caught up with her.

"Sunday dinner?"

She glanced back over one shoulder. Should she?

He uncrossed his arms. "No strings attached."

If he only knew how wrong he was. "What time?"

"Around one, but I can pick you up at ten thirty. Take you to church and to the folks' after."

The church invitation threw her. The Buchanons were pillars of Christ's Church, where she attended when she could, but she'd never seen Quinn there.

Had the Lord orchestrated this moment to get Quinn back into the congregation? Or, she inwardly mocked, maybe she was looking for an excuse to be with him. "What can I bring?"

Quinn hooked his good arm around Derrick's neck. "Yourself and this little twerp."

With a nod, stomach lurching and uncertainty her middle name, she left them standing there together, father and son who didn't know.

"Better get back on the field." Quinn unwound his arm from Derrick's neck and watched the boy jog away, but his thoughts were on Gena. He probably shouldn't have invited her to dinner, didn't want to be at the Buchanon get-together, but he wanted to be with her and couldn't seem to help himself.

The pills must be destroying his mental acuity. Pretty

soon he'd be a babbling idiot, begging on the street corner with a cardboard sign.

He was a mess.

While he wasn't fit to be in church, he needed God more right now than ever.

He had to get free. Every time he screwed up the courage to go cold turkey, the nerves in his arm sent hot fire into his shoulder and he fell off the wagon again. Shame and regret hung on him like a sweaty shirt.

Tonight he'd try again to pull an all-nighter without the pills. Yesterday he'd made it to midnight. Tonight he'd make it to dawn, even if he had to take a boat out on the river and toss the oars overboard.

He was deep in thought, but the rumble of young voices breaking with adolescence drew his attention away from his problems. With Derrick in the lead, swaggering some to boot, they came at him like something out of a movie.

He hadn't been near a football field in twelve years and had wondered why he'd been compelled to watch Derrick's practice today. Looking at the kid's face, he knew. He'd come for the boy with a wad of hurt bigger than his own.

A swarm of sweaty youths encircled him, curious and admiring. If they only knew he was not a man to admire.

"You're him. I thought Derrick was lying." This from a dark-haired boy the size of a young rhino.

"Offensive line?" he asked the kid.

The boy's mouth gaped open. "Guard. Wow. How did you know?"

Another boy, number eighty-six, gave Rhino Boy a push. "He's Quinn Buchanon, man. Don't you think he knows football better than anybody?"

The damaged arm wasn't visible, but Quinn figured if he removed the jacket, they'd all gasp in horror and then disappear faster than Gatorade after a hot practice. He wouldn't be impressive then.

"My dad said you were some kind of a hotshot. Is that right?"

"Long time ago, boys."

"Yeah, but GC hasn't won a state championship since you played. My dad says you were like some kind of superhuman in that game. Crazy good."

He remembered.

"Tell us about the last drive, when the Tigers were down by a touchdown with only a minute and a half left."

Uncomfortable but flattered, too, Quinn shook his head. "Your dad has a good memory. Ask him."

"Aw, Quinn, come on," Derrick said. "Tell them."

From the light in Derrick's eyes, this was the most positive attention he'd had since moving to Gabriel's Crossing. These were his peers, and he was the city kid who didn't fit in.

"All right." He moved into their huddle as he had in the championship game and related the final drive, play by play. The boys listened with rapt attention.

When he finished, he said, "Without my O line protecting me—" he tapped Rhino Boy on the helmet and the kid preened "—receivers to catch my passes and a hard-hitting defense that kept us in the game, I'd have been toast."

"But your pass into the end zone for the two-point conversion. My dad said nobody else could have made that throw against a blitzing defense."

Sports commentators had touted the pass as impossible. Across his body to the opposite side of the field and on the run with a defensive back hanging on his ankle. He couldn't remember if he'd been desperate or determined. Likely both.

"Can you show us some stuff?" another boy asked. "Like you do Derrick?"

"You have a coach for that, boys."

"Coach won't care. He's cool."

"I'll pass."

"Give him the ball. He said he'd pass." Number eighty-six chortled, proud of his joke.

"Man." Rhino Boy elbowed the speaker. "Not cool, Harris. Don't you remember? His arm got destroyed. He can't throw anymore."

While Quinn floundered, humiliated and miserable, Gena's voice spun him around. "Sure he can. He throws with Derrick."

Quinn leveled her with a frown. "I thought you left."

"Emergency canceled and I'm off the rest of the day. I thought Derrick might want a ride home after practice." She crossed her arms and gave him a stare-down. "Are you going to show the boys some stuff or make excuses?"

"They have a coach."

"A coach who has more players than he has time." The coach stuck out a hand. "How you doing, Buchanon? Long time."

Quinn hadn't even noticed the coach on the edge of the huddle, a man he'd known in high school. "Grant, good to see you."

"Coach, you don't mind if he shows us some plays, do you?" To Quinn, number eight said, "I'm a QB, like you. I'm pretty good but you're a legend. Can you make me better?"

Coach Richardson's smile challenged him. "What do you say, Quinn?"

Quinn rotated his right arm as far as possible, which wasn't far enough. "I don't know…"

"You're a football mind, Quinn," Gena stunned him by saying. "You don't need your arm to impart knowledge. Right, Coach?"

"I can't kick a field goal but I can teach a kid to kick one." Coach laughed. "Tell you what. Why don't you hang around and watch? If the spirit moves, jump in."

The smell of a football field filled Quinn's lungs and carried him back to a better time. Grass and dirt. Sweat and leather. Energy and excitement. The only thing missing was the fear, a smell he'd thrived on when he'd lined up against an opposing player who dreaded facing his arm.

There was no smell on earth he loved more than a football field. He itched to be back out there.

But his shoulder nagged from that one small rotation, reminding him of what he couldn't do.

He looked from Gena's challenging stare to forty eager faces, one in particular. The twerp appeared ready to levitate. Another second and he'd take flight. Dumb kid. Dumb, hurting kid.

What could he say? He slapped number eight on the back.

"Get out there and show me what you got."

Chapter Ten

Church service with Quinn was far different from a service by herself. The Buchanon family took up an entire pew by themselves and spilled over into the next one. Bracketed on either side by a very large, handsome male, Gena worked hard to focus on the uplifting service. Derrick perched on the other side of Quinn, although he tried his best to look as if the seating was accidental.

Quinn's right shoulder brushed hers and occasionally throughout the service he rubbed it, whether from habit or pain, she didn't know, but she was concerned.

He was resplendently handsome dressed up in a pale green shirt with navy striped tie that matched navy slacks. He took her breath, a silly female thought, but there it was. Even an egghead got flutters when the man of her girlhood dreams sat next to her, his baritone softly singing the words displayed on an overhead screen.

The minister spoke on trusting God through the hard times and she jotted notes in her purse-sized spiral notepad. Once, Quinn leaned over and whispered, "There won't be a test."

She smiled at his gentle teasing, and her throat clutched at the closeness of their faces.

"You never know," she said.

His gaze lingered too long and Gena couldn't turn away until he did. Later she prayed that God would give her direction in this tangled mess with Quinn.

When church concluded, they filed through the crowd, stopping to greet friends and some of her patients. Everyone knew Quinn and some expressed pleasure that he was there. He looked both pleased and embarrassed.

"Quinn." One man stopped him with an outstretched hand. "My son, Sean, plays for the middle school. He said you dropped in on a practice."

"That's right." Quinn's expression wasn't a happy one, as if he expected the man to bring up his arm, the accident, his inabilities.

But the other man simply said, "Thanks for doing that. The boys were pumped, from what I'm told. Sean talked of little else that night."

"No problem." With a nod that barely fell short of abrupt, Quinn took her hand and eased out into the cloudy day. For a man who was once a glory hound basking in the pages of *Sports Illustrated*, praise made him miserable.

Derrick was already in the backseat of Quinn's truck, but the door stood open and he chatted to a blonde girl near his age. Milly Something, she thought. As soon as she spotted the adults, the girl walked away, waving, and Derrick slammed the door.

Gena exchanged a silent smile with Quinn and stepped up into the pickup.

The Buchanon house was only blocks away from the church and a parade of cars pulled into the drive and along the curb out front. People tumbled out and went inside the large split-level home—Buchanon Built, of course, and a real showplace.

Quinn exited the truck much slower than the rest and lingered in the yard.

"Everything all right?" she asked.

"I haven't been here since Christmas."

"Why not?"

He barked a short, mirthless laugh. "Stupidity."

"You're here now." She hooked her elbow with his, and they went inside, where so many voices spoke at once that at first she couldn't discern a one.

But with Quinn at her side and Derrick already disappeared into the backyard with Charity's son, Ryan, Gena soon made the rounds. In the kitchen, the Buchanon women—mom, Karen; sisters Allison, Charity and Jaylee, along with Abby—crowded the enormous bar with food and chatter.

"Quinny!" Allison squealed and rushed over to wrap her arms around Quinn's waist. A diminutive woman smaller than Derrick, Allison was the bubbly-cheerleader type. Gena treated her at the clinic. "Gena, thank you for bringing him. We miss his cranky face."

Quinn put extra effort into his scowl. "Be useful and bring me a glass of tea."

She stuck out her tongue and threw a dishtowel at him. The other women laughed.

"No respect." But his eyes danced when he said it. If he was anxious about being here, he hid his tension well.

He led her into the den, where March Madness played on a flat-screen television that took up half the wall.

"Do you like basketball?" he asked.

"I was a geek in school, remember? I didn't do sports. And now I don't have that much time."

"You know football."

Because of you. "A little."

Five other males and Brady's dog sprawled over the living room. She recognized all of them, but hadn't been formally introduced to anyone but Brady.

Brady saluted her. Allison's husband, Jake, nodded even though his gaze kept returning to the kitchen, where his dark-haired wife talked a mile a minute. Charity's absent husband, she learned, was a pilot on his second deployment with the military.

"These are the twins, Dawson with the dimple and Sawyer, the leftie."

Sawyer slapped a hand against his chest. "Nurse! Nurse! Emergency. I need a nurse."

Gena laughed at a joke she'd heard dozens of times. "I'll schedule you for a colonoscopy and get back to you."

The other men hooted and Sawyer pretended hurt, though his blue eyes sparkled.

"Better grab her, Quinn. She's not only smarter than you, she's the only woman I've ever met who prefers you over me." He shook his dark head. "I'm in shock."

Gena laughed, feeling good in the company of this wonderful, fun-loving family.

"And I'm the cause of all these troublemakers." Dan Buchanon, kicked back in a leather recliner, waved at her across the room. "Have a seat and we'll teach you the finer points of basketball."

"I should help in the kitchen." She bumped Quinn's arm and gazed pointedly at the men. "So should you male chauvinists."

Abby came out of the kitchen area to open the patio doors for Lila and her walker. "We cook. The guys clean up. No chauvinists allowed in Karen's household."

"Really? I'm impressed."

"See why I don't come over here more often?" Quinn asked. "Mom makes me work. But you're a guest. You get to stay in here with us."

The invitation tempted, but she wanted to make a good impression and she also wanted to know the Buchanon women better. Maybe they could give her some insight into her neighbor. She certainly needed all the help she could get to understand Quinn Buchanon.

Though reluctant to leave Quinn, she went into the kitchen and asked, "How can I help?"

Karen, Quinn's blonde mother, pointed to several covered bowls on the counter. "Those need to be heated in the microwave and put on the table."

"I can do that."

"Quinn tells me you're teaching yourself to cook with your grandmother's recipes. Anna was a fabulous cook."

"He told you that?"

One of Karen's eyebrows lifted. "He did."

Allison arranged strawberries on top of a white cake. "He's talked about you a lot lately. I think he's smitten."

"Oh, no. We're just…neighbors." *And I can't fall in love with him. I'm not even supposed to like him.*

Then what was she doing here?

Karen rested her wrists against a bowl and smiled. "Quinn has never shown interest in a neighbor before." Then she sobered. "You're an answer to prayer, Gena. I had despaired of ever getting him back in church."

"He hasn't been since the accident." Jaylee, thin as a tongue depressor with pale blond waist-length hair, arranged a tray of fresh veggies. "We've all been worried, but he hates having us pry into his business."

"Which doesn't stop us." Allison laughed. "Now that he's seeing you, you can be our spy."

Though Allison joked, Gena didn't like the notion of spying on anyone. If Quinn had a prescription drug problem, he didn't want them to know, and as a medical professional, she respected privacy. Her lips were sealed. "He lets Derrick feed his kittens."

"According to Quinn, they aren't his kittens. He hates cats."

A small smile crooked her lips. "I know. He works hard to be Mr. Tough Guy." She glanced toward the living room, where Brady and Quinn were in deep conversation. "I think he's really a soft touch."

"As a kid, he was as sensitive as Dawson. On the football field he had to display toughness." Karen frowned over a bowl of mashed potatoes. "I'm not sure that was a good thing."

"Maybe," Allison mused, "that's why the injury sent him into such depression for so long."

"Among other things that happened around that time," Karen answered.

Gena waited for her to elaborate but she didn't. What other things had cut so deep that he still struggled to find peace?

The microwave beeped and Gena traded out casserole dishes, taking the heated one to the enormous rectangular table already laden with food. Stepping to the window, she glanced out at Derrick and Ryan. The two boys tossed a football back and forth, chatting.

A good feeling settled over her. The change in Derrick was slow, but he was making friends and showing interest in something other than his gangbanger friends. Last night while he'd been at Quinn's cabin, she'd checked his Facebook. He hadn't posted anything in days.

Karen came up beside her and followed her gaze to the two boys. In a quiet voice, she said, "I was so terribly sorry to hear about Renae."

Gena swallowed. "Thank you."

"Derrick is her son?"

"Yes." Renae's son. Quinn's son.

Her conscience did battle as if two opposing teams fought for dominance inside her head. On the one hand was a promise to her dying sister and the beloved child Renae had entrusted to her care. On the other was the Buchanons, an incredible Christian family filled with love and relationships that she alone couldn't give to her nephew.

Which was worse? To keep his parentage secret from these good people? Or to break a deathbed promise and risk losing Derrick altogether?

Who was she kidding? Nothing had changed. Things weren't looking up at all.

"Today was a good day." Quinn opened the passenger door for Gena and held her hand as she stepped down. Considering she was a medical professional whose hands took a beating, her skin felt soft against his rough, much larger hand.

"Your family is so warm and welcoming. I enjoyed them."

"You handled my brothers pretty well. They were impressed."

"I like guys who joke around."

"Yeah, well, I'll polish my stand-up routine."

Gena laughed, and pleasure bubbled up in Quinn.

"You have a beautiful laugh," he said, sounding like the old Quinn instead of himself. Compliment the girls and they'd fall all over him. The memory made him scowl. Quinn the Mighty was history.

"And you have a beautiful smile. You just need to use it more."

Derrick slammed out of the backseat. "You're gagging me. I'll be in the shed."

Both adults grinned. Quinn called to the retreating boy. "The kittens are eating solid food now. They don't need us anymore, Derrick."

"Yeah, they do." The shed opened and shut as Derrick disappeared inside.

"Would you like to see them?" Quinn asked. "They've grown a lot."

He'd used the kittens as an excuse to stop at the cabin

before taking Gena home. They'd had a good day and he was reluctant to let her go.

Yes, he was pathetic. The old Quinn wouldn't have needed a reason. He would have simply assumed she couldn't bear to be away from him. Arrogant sucker.

"I'd love to. Derrick's attached to them."

"They're good for him." Him, too, but he wouldn't admit that.

"What will you do with them when they're completely weaned?"

"I don't know." The question irritated him. "Give them away, I suppose. Want one?"

"Maybe." She laughed. "Derrick will want all of them but that is not happening."

They walked together to the shed, unhurried. He'd been careful with the pills today and had himself under control. "Church was good. I hadn't been in a while. Good message."

Getting through the hard times. He hadn't done so well in that department. So far.

"You have a nice singing voice."

He beamed at her. "So do you." High and sweet.

They paused beside the shed, a slight March breeze chilling the air around them, but warmth emanated from their smiles. Before he could think better of it, he leaned in and kissed her lightly.

She didn't seem to mind.

"Thanks for going with me today." He took her hand and pulled it into his chest. "You made being there easier."

"To church or to your parents' house?"

"Both."

Her head tilted. "Why have you avoided them?"

Guilt. Respect. Fear of failing them all over again. "I don't know."

"Will you go again next Sunday?"

"Will you go with me?" Something inexplicable shifted on the breeze and Quinn desperately wanted her to say yes. He needed her in his life, as wrong as that would be at this point in time. "You're good for me, Gena."

And he was bad for her. Lousy bad. An unselfish man would send her away while he could.

Another failure on his part.

Emotions flickered across her face like a sixteen-millimeter film. "Derrick—"

"Church is good for him, too. I'll throw a kitten into the deal if you say yes."

She smiled. "You drive a hard bargain."

"So what do you say? You, me, Derrick, church."

Her smile widened, and she didn't pull her hand away. Instead she tugged him toward the shed door. "Let's have a look at those kittens."

Chapter Eleven

Quinn dropped by football practice twice more in the next two weeks. Being there both thrilled and depressed him. There was no way he could attend the first scrimmage, even though Derrick hinted that he wanted him there.

Derrick. Gena.

Somehow his neighbors had become ensconced in his daily routine, and the more time he spent with them, the less time he spent thinking about the next dose of oxycodone. That was a good thing. Something to cling to. Something to build on.

God worked in mysterious ways, he supposed, and he prayed every day and every night and twice on Sunday that he could lay the pills down altogether. Only then would he have a right to involve other people in his life. Not just anyone, but Gena.

Right or not, he couldn't stay away from her. The fact that she liked him, too, broke down his resistance faster than sweat dries in the Sahara.

Even though the kittens no longer required bottle feedings and they'd forgone the midnight meetings, Derrick showed up at the cabin after school like clockwork, and Quinn had developed a habit of tossing the bike in the back of his truck and driving the kid home. Usually, Gena was there and he stayed until the pain called his name.

Yesterday afternoon he'd gotten hung up at work because some joker had dumped paint all over the outside brick of a new house in the Huckleberry Addition. He and his brothers and Dad had thought the vandalism was behind them after Abby's house burned to the ground. He hoped the paint incident was unrelated but he wouldn't count on it. Not after the note Brady had found at Abby's burned home. Someone had a personal vendetta. The lingering questions remained. Who and why?

Today he pumped the handles of his elliptical cross-trainer, running and exercising while he waited on Derrick. The kid was late. But Quinn could use the extra workout.

He was soaked with sweat and gritting his teeth against the ache when he heard the bike clatter against the wooden porch. He punched the machine's off button and grabbed a towel.

Wiping his face and feeling accomplished, he opened the door. Derrick slumped inside, his hood up.

Uh-oh.

He gestured toward the couch. "Sit. I gotta grab some water. Want some?"

Derrick shook his head no and slouched onto the sofa.

Quinn filled a sport bottle, slung the towel around his neck and perched across from the boy. "Spill it."

Derrick glanced up and back down. He pulled a photo from his pouch. "Today's my mom's birthday."

Quinn's belly dipped. If he'd ever known the date, he'd forgotten.

Totally out of his element, he searched for something kind and useful to say. "You miss her."

Stupid. Of course an eleven-year-old boy missed his mother.

No matter what Renae had done to him, he ached for the grieving boy. "I know."

Suddenly, as if he knew what he was doing, Quinn moved to the couch next to Derrick. He'd no more than made the transition when the boy tilted against him, sobbing.

Awkward, uncertain, but touched by the boy's grief, Quinn patted his back and slowly let his arm settle around the lanky shoulders. Derrick was a kid. A boy. A child. His understanding of life was small, but his sorrow was enormous.

"They should have told me," Derrick sobbed. "No one told me."

This was the second time the boy had made that statement. This time Quinn wanted to know. "Told you what, bud?"

The young body shuddered as he fought for composure. Finally, in a breathless, broken voice, he managed, "They said she'd be okay. They said not to worry. They sent me out. I was playing a stupid video game while my mom died! I didn't even get to say goodbye!"

Oh man. No wonder the kid was angry.

"Ah, Derrick." Quinn stroked up and down the boy's back, sick at heart and as helpless as those baby kittens had been. He was the worst person in the world to counsel a troubled, angry soul.

But he was the only one here. For whatever reason, the kid had picked him to trust with his heartache.

The responsibility pressed down on Quinn.

"Why did she have to die?" Derrick straightened, cheeks tear streaked and eyes red. Face set in tight lines of fury, he dashed at the tears with a sleeve. "Why did God let that happen? Why?"

Good question, God.

"I wish I had an answer, buddy. Sometimes life deals

you a lousy hand." Experience was a harsh teacher. "You have to make the most of your life anyway."

Derrick drew back and glared. In a sarcastic tone, he said, "Yeah? Like you did?"

Quinn had never been good at platitudes.

Derrick's words stung, mostly because they were true. Nearly twelve years after life had dealt the Mighty Quinn a lousy hand, he still brooded and moped and whined. Self-pity was his best friend.

God forgive me.

The time had come for Mighty Quinn to put the past to rest.

But today wasn't about him. Today, this moment, was about this brokenhearted, motherless, fatherless boy.

How would he have survived the last twelve years without the love and support of his parents? Even when he rejected them, they'd remained steady and faithful.

He rose from the sofa, dug a Mountain Dew from the refrigerator, popped the top and handed the can to Derrick. Shoulders stooped, appearing for all the world like a windup toy that had run down, the boy took the soda but didn't sip.

Quinn went to his knees in front of Derrick so that they were eye to eye. The kid was going to be big someday.

"Platitudes don't cut it, Derrick. You're right about that. Losing your mom is the worst thing that will ever happen to you. Life won't ever be the same again. The hurt will ease but the grief won't ever completely leave." Quinn shuddered in a breath. Truth was hard but better than smooth words without meaning.

Sad blue eyes lifted to his. Renae's eyes. "Will I ever stop feeling so...so..." He floundered for a word.

"Angry? Helpless? Brokenhearted?"

Derrick licked his lips and nodded. "Yeah."

"I don't know," Quinn answered honestly. "I think that's

"Yeah." Derrick sniffed. "I thought…" He stopped, shuddered, and his chest heaved.

Panic pushed up in Quinn's throat. Was Derrick crying? What was he supposed to do with a crying kid?

He gulped half the bottle of water. The refrigerator clicked on, loud in the silent cabin. Quinn cleared his throat.

Floundering but desperate to do *something*, he gently tapped the photo. "Is this your mom?"

Derrick nodded and turned the photo toward Quinn.

Like he was a punctured football, all the wind whooshed out of him.

"She was beautiful," he managed when he regained his breath. Gorgeous. He still couldn't believe Renae was dead.

Memories tumbled in of the bright, vibrant brunette who had turned his world upside down. He'd loved her as much as he could love anyone during those wild days on top of the world. Then, while he was in the hospital with his whole world shattered along with his arm, she'd walked away. She didn't visit. She didn't call. Not once. She'd left him with a load of resentment and helped convince him that without the golden arm, women weren't interested. No one wanted him.

"I imagine she was a great mother," he said.

He couldn't imagine any such thing. Renae was a flirt, a girl who loved the nightlife and parties and lots of attention. His hadn't been enough, not after the accident.

"She made me chocolate chip pancakes on my birthday. I always promised to make her some when I got big. Breakfast in bed with coffee and everything." A fat tear dripped on the picture. "I would have done it this year, Quinn. Gena taught me. I wish—" A sob broke free.

"I know, buddy." Sympathy curled up inside him and throttled his heart, squeezing until he, too, wanted to cry.

up to you. But you'll always miss her. You'll always love her and wish she was here. I imagine birthdays and holidays will be the worst. One thing I know for sure, Derrick, if you hold on to the bad feelings, they'll eat you alive."

He was living, breathing proof of that, fool that he was.

"I don't know how to stop."

He didn't, either. "We have to try. Both of us."

"Gena prays."

"Me, too."

"You?"

"I'm getting back into it. Maybe we both should."

"I guess."

"Your family didn't mean to leave you out. That day at the hospital. They were trying to protect you."

"Yeah. I guess." Derrick heaved a heavy sigh, stared at the soda for a second, then raised the can and took a sip. "I'm gonna go see the kittens. Optimus waits at the door for me."

He set the soda on the end table, pocketed the photo of Renae and started out.

"Derrick," Quinn said.

Derrick turned, lanky arms hanging loose at his sides. "Yeah."

"Maybe we could do something to commemorate today. A birthday's special."

"Like what?"

"I have a package of Hostess cupcakes." Stupid idea. "One for you. One for me. Both for her."

The boy's expression lit with interest. "You got candles?"

Candles. Why hadn't he thought before he shot off his big mouth? He considered for a second or two and then lifted an index finger. "Matches. And we'll both sing."

"Okay." Derrick almost smiled. "Mom would laugh."

Yeah. She would have. *Happy birthday, Renae.*

* * *

Later that night, Gena listened with a heavy heart as Quinn shared Derrick's breakdown and the sweet, heart-rending celebration he'd orchestrated with two cupcakes and a pair of stick matches.

That her nephew had chosen Quinn as his venting outlet surprised her, though perhaps it shouldn't have.

The two of them sat together on the front porch of the Satterfield home in a green metal glider that had been there for years. Derrick had gone to bed early and now she understood why. He was emotionally spent and probably embarrassed at crying in front of his football hero.

March pushed toward April and while days grew pleasant, evenings remained cool. Gena arranged a soft throw across their knees the way Nana had always done. She visualized Nana in this exact spot, shelling peas or mending Papa's socks or, better yet, sharing a story with her two granddaughters. This was home, a healing place. At least, she hoped it would be for Derrick. Herself, as well.

"That's the first time he's cried about her."

Quinn sat close, his large body warm against the chill. "Not even at the funeral?"

"Not even then. We were worried because he seemed withdrawn…indifferent almost."

"Shock?"

"I'm sure that was part of his reaction, and then when the anger and acting out began, I knew he was in trouble." She gnawed at the edge of her thumbnail. "But he wouldn't talk and he didn't cry. We couldn't seem to reach him."

Quinn shifted, his knee brushing hers. "We?"

"My parents and I."

"What about his father?"

Her heart stuttered. She glanced away and back again. "He wasn't in the picture.'"

True enough, though he was now.

Quickly, before he pried deeper, she went on. "Derrick started skipping school, hanging out with the wrong people, failing classes. When he was arrested for shoplifting, I knew I had to make a change."

"Gabriel's Crossing is glad you did."

Her shoulders lifted. "Dr. Ramos is a family friend and had asked me to consider relocating when I first graduated with my CRNP. I thought Gabriel's Crossing was God's answer to my prayers."

"And now?"

A slippery slope and one she did not want to go down. "He's better. The fact that he opened up to you is major."

"He misses her. And he doesn't understand."

She tilted her head, taking in the sculpted profile and Buchanon bone structure that turned female heads, including hers and Renae's. Had he missed Renae the way Renae had missed him? "I know."

"What about you? You must miss her badly. The two of you were real close."

"You remember that?"

"I remember a lot of things, Gena."

Fear shot an arrow through her heart. What kind of things?

While she grappled, afraid of discovery, he went on. "She thought you were the smartest person in the world."

He found her hand beneath the blanket and lifted her fingers one by one. "She was incredibly proud of you but also intimidated by you."

"Me?" Gena closed her hand, afraid of the tingles running from his skin to hers, afraid of the feelings she could not control or deny. Tonight especially, when she, like Derrick, was vulnerable with memories of Renae. "My sister was the bright star."

"Renae didn't see it that way. To her you were the one with the big future. You should have heard her brag." He took her hand again and this time she didn't withdraw. "Gena got straight As again. Gena won a scholarship, a full ride! Gena graduated magna cum laude."

"She said all that?"

"How else would I know you got the highest A in Comparative Anatomy?"

The news stunned her. She'd been the nerdy, brainy sister, the socially awkward tagalong. Renae never noticed what she did.

Her heart ballooned. Renae *had* noticed.

"All this time I thought…" The words faded away. As much as she'd loved Renae, she'd envied her, too. How many times had she wished she could trade her brains for Renae's popularity and beauty? Or wished to be the girl on Quinn's arm instead of her sister?

"You thought what?"

"Never mind." Tears pushed at the back of her eyelids. "She was a great sister. The best. I wish I could tell her one more time how much I loved her."

"She knew."

Grateful, she blinked up at him. "Thank you."

He touched her cheek. "Don't cry."

"I'm not." But a tear leaked out and called her a liar.

Quinn wiped the moisture away with his thumb but another followed. She seldom cried. As a medical professional, she kept her emotions in check.

But the tears seemed to have a mind of their own.

"I don't know why I'm suddenly emotional. This is silly."

"Today is her birthday. She's on your mind. You miss her. Derrick misses her. Nothing wrong with that." A strong pair of arms encircled her. "Come here. I have big shoulders."

He did indeed.

Gena required little coaxing. She rested her cheek

against his chest. His heart beat a steady, determined rhythm in her ear, a contrast to her wild and fluttering arrhythmia.

Comforted, soothed and protected. How could she feel so cared for in the arms of her sister's betrayer?

What was she going to do about Quinn Buchanon?

Quinn paced the floor of the cabin. Last night had opened his eyes. He'd thought of little else today at work. He'd been so distracted Dad had told him to go home and get some sleep.

Sleep wasn't what he needed.

He was a selfish jerk. Not because of the pills that had taken over his life but because he'd used his arm as an excuse to dull his senses with a narcotic. Sure, the old injury hurt, sometimes worse than others, but he had never meant for things to get out of hand.

Going to the cabinet, he took down the latest refill of oxycodone. Chronic pain burned from elbow to shoulder. One pill and the pain eased. Two or three, and he could forget his arm, forget the loss, forget everything.

After an evening with Gena, he didn't want to forget anymore. He wanted to remember the way she felt in his arms and the smell of her hair and the way hope rose inside him hot and desperate.

Life the way he'd been living it was not enough.

He closed his hand around the bottle, dwarfing the narrow plastic vial.

Every day, he vowed not to take a single caplet. Every day, he failed. Even on the nights when he ran the river and prayed not to succumb, he didn't see dawn without at least one.

He was legal, a fact he'd clung to as an excuse. If the pills were legally prescribed by his doctor, they couldn't hurt him. He wouldn't become dependent. A self-destructive lie. He didn't buy them on the street, but he couldn't stop taking them, either. Would he someday stoop to street-corner transactions?

Derrick looked up to him. He trusted him with his heart and his heartache. Quinn wanted to be a good role model. Most of all, he wanted to be a man worthy of the way Gena had looked at him last night when she'd cried on his shoulder.

He glanced at the clock above his range. Gena would be home soon. If he was half the man he wanted to be, he'd do this thing.

He raised his eyes to the ceiling. "God, I'm going to need Your help."

Grabbing his keys, he drove to the Satterfield farm. Gena's Xterra sat under the carport. His gut lurched, an early warning of what was to come.

He slammed out of the truck and jogged up to the porch. Gena opened the door before he knocked.

"Hi." Her smile welcomed him.

Quinn swallowed the butterflies. "Is Derrick home?"

"Football practice and then he's going over to Ryan's."

Awesome. He didn't want the twerp around for this ugly business. "Charity's son?"

"They hit it off pretty well Sunday."

"Ryan's ornery but a decent kid. Charity keeps a close eye on him. He'll make a good friend."

"I think so, too." She stepped back, holding the door open. "Want to come in?"

The butterflies were back. "Yeah. We need to talk."

Gena got a strange, cautious expression on her face but nodded and led him through the homey living room into the kitchen.

"When they were alive, Nana and Papa talked best around the kitchen table," she said. "Want some tea?"

"Thanks." He looked at his hands spread on the scarred

wooden table and contemplated what he was about to do. If he told her, asked for her expertise, would she be repulsed? Would this be the end of a relationship that had barely begun?

She placed two filled glasses on the table and sat, folding her hands on top, directly across from his. He dwarfed her.

He cleared his throat and said, "I need some medical advice."

Her breath exhaled softly as if she'd expected something else. "All right, but I do have an office."

"This is private. I don't want anyone else to know."

Green, green eyes lifted to his and held on. She was smart. She'd figure out the problem if she hadn't already.

"How bad is the pain, Quinn?"

Shame suffused him. He didn't know if he could go through with telling her everything, but he was alone in the cabin. Anything could happen. Shouldn't someone he trusted know what he was about to do?

"Some days are worse than others. The nights are killers."

"You don't sleep well?"

He huffed a short, self-mocking sound. "No."

"Because of the pain…or the pills?"

He swallowed, shaky inside for reasons that had nothing to do with either pain or pills. Last night she'd admired the way he'd handled the situation with Derrick. He didn't want to disappoint her or to see her admiration drain away to pity, or worse, to nothing at all.

A sigh escaped him but he felt no relief.

He wrapped his fingers around the prescription bottle in his pocket. He should take it out, lay his problem on the table and walk away. That had been his intention.

He released the bottle and withdrew his hand.

He couldn't do this. Not yet. Not this way. Not with Gena.

Pushing out of his chair, he said, "Look. Never mind. Okay. I…uh… I wanted you to know I'm going out of town for a few days. Tell Derrick I won't be at the cabin, but I've left plenty of cat food."

She reached out and caught his hand, holding him rooted to her kitchen floor. "Let's talk about your pain, Quinn. Have you spoken with your doctor about how bad it is?"

"It's not that big of a deal. I'm okay." He forced a grin. "Really. I'll talk with my Dallas docs. I'm heading up there." Not a lie. He *was* going to Dallas. In about three weeks.

He could see she didn't believe him.

Still holding his fingers in hers, she rose, puzzled but with such compassion he almost changed his mind. Again.

"If you're not sleeping and the pain is chronic, ask about pain management. I can help you with that."

"Sure. Sounds good." He backed away, breaking contact. "We'll talk after I see the surgeon."

Eager to escape before he spilled his guts all over her antiseptically clean kitchen, he moved to the front door. Why had he thought this was a good idea?

Trying to be casual, he said, "Derrick will look after the cats?"

"That goes without saying."

"Great. I'll let you know when I get back."

Her lips curved, though a pinch remained between her eyebrows, a sign that her brain hadn't quite let go of something. "We'll miss you."

"Same here." He kissed her lightly but enough to rock his world. She did that to him, and because she did, he couldn't let her down.

On the way back to the cabin, he called his less-than-happy dad with the news that he was taking a week's vacation in Dallas starting tomorrow.

Now to figure out what to do with his truck. Derrick would come to the cabin every day. Quinn didn't want him knocking on the door.

The websites and forums claimed a week was enough to detox. He prayed they were right.

Whatever, as Derrick would say. He was on his own.

Chapter Twelve

For five straight days Gena wrestled with the bizarre conversation. Quinn had wanted to share something with her but had changed his mind. Though he'd eschewed her concern, she remained convinced. The problem was serious.

Had he been ready to discuss the pills he claimed not to take although she knew he did? She'd watched his eyes and recognized when his pupils constricted to pinpoints and he seemed more relaxed and easy. Did he have a problem? Was he dependent? Only he knew the answer, and he didn't trust her enough to confide.

Every day, she rang his cell phone, though she knew he only answered when he wanted to talk. Which, apparently, he didn't. She had, however, expected him to return the calls at his convenience. That he didn't stung, and the sudden silence also worried her.

Something was definitely amiss. All her warning bells clanged. Every medical instinct she'd honed warned her that Quinn needed help but was too proud to ask.

"I wonder when he's coming back." Derrick flopped into a chair and pointed the remote at the TV. He'd arrived home a few minutes ago from his daily visit with the kittens and reported, to her disappointment, that Quinn's truck had not returned.

Gena looked up from her device. Updating patient charts never ended, even when she was home. "Who?"

"You know who. Quinn."

"Not our business." Though it pained her to admit that. She wanted to know and worried that he was unwell or worse. "He said a few days, maybe a week." She hit Save and put the device aside. "Hungry?"

He shot her a bored look. "Does an owl hoot? Do birds chirp?"

"Country slang. Nice. I think the city boy is fading."

A snarky grin slashed his face. "Houston wasn't all that great."

"No?"

"My school didn't start football until middle school. GC has Little League. I could have played if I'd been here then. Did you know that?"

"If I did, I'd forgotten." Carefully, knowing she trod on shaky ground, she probed. "How are your friends in Houston doing?"

A shoulder jerked. "Don't know. I dumped them."

Thank You, sweet Jesus! "What brought about this sudden change of heart?"

"Ah, you know. Stuff. Quinn said gangbangers are dead-end. They never get football scholarships."

A mix of anxiety and hope stirred in Gena. Hope that her nephew was finally finding safe footing. Fear that Derrick and Quinn were too much alike.

DNA was a powerful thing. Why hadn't she considered that the day she'd discovered Quinn was her neighbor? "Is football your goal?"

"Maybe. I gotta get better, work hard. They won't give scholarships for my good looks, no matter how pretty I am," he chortled. "Quinn said he knew because he tried."

She laughed, too, although she worried about all the Quinn references. Like father, like son, they were both talented and handsome and sarcastically funny. She saw the similarities. Sooner or later, someone else would do the same.

"How are the kitties?"

"Bored. Like me right now. They want out of that shed. When I'm there we play in the yard, but if I leave them outside, coyotes might get them."

Gena was pleased by the responsibility he'd displayed with the kittens. He was still mouthy and moody, but he was doing so much better she could almost relax. Except for Quinn.

"Which one are you going to keep? Optimus?"

"I guess."

"Why don't you bring him home with you tomorrow?"

He gave her a sidelong look as if wondering what planet she was from. "What about the others? They're all cute and sweet." He flashed a fake grin. "Like me."

She held up a finger. "One. And one only."

"Can't blame a guy for trying." He clicked off the muted TV and tossed the remote aside. "Can I go over to Ryan's? He might want a kitten."

That he asked permission was another giant step of progress. In Houston he'd simply disappear. "I'll call Charity and make sure you aren't wearing out your welcome."

"Will you drive me into town?"

"If she says it's okay. But only for a couple of hours. I have a few things to do at the clinic anyway."

And she was going to try one more time to reach Quinn.

He felt weaker than chicken broth, a substance that he tried to keep in his stomach for the first time in days. Today was better. The aches and weakness still kept him glued to the couch or the bed most of the time, but the stomach issues had eased. Not enough that Quinn dared throw a steak on the grill, but he thought he might live.

He hadn't slept much since the ordeal began and when he did, the dreams scared him awake.

He'd never prayed so much in his life. Short, desperate, begging prayers. On his knees. On the floor. In the bathroom.

Oxycodone was a mean master that didn't want to let go.

After six months of eight to ten a day, sometimes more, he'd lived five whole days and nights without a single dose. If you could call what he'd been through living.

He licked dry, dry lips and swallowed a spoonful of broth. When the salty liquid stayed down, he tried another and another. The spoon shook and he lost as much as he ingested.

His cell phone buzzed, dancing on the end table next to the couch.

Gena again.

He'd plugged in the device as a precaution in case he reached the point of death. Detox had tried. But he'd won.

He hadn't won in a long, long time. Later, when he wasn't exhausted, the victory would feel good.

She'd called him every day. And every day, he wanted to answer, if only to hear her beautiful voice. Instead he listened to the voice mails, and her calls reminded him of the good that waited on the other side of this battle.

The ringing stopped. His heart sank. She hadn't left a message this time. Had she given up on him? Was she mad because he hadn't returned her calls?

He pushed up on shaky legs, then carried the empty cup to the sink and took a bottle of Gatorade from the fridge. On the football field, the sport drink had eased dehydration. Might as well keep it handy to sip now that he could.

He pulled back the curtain over the kitchen window and looked out for the first time in five days. Dusk gathered in sparkling gray shimmers that hovered over a yellow burst of daffodils his sisters had planted in his backyard. An owl flapped to a landing in the lone sycamore tree, yellow luminescent eyes catching the ambient light.

The world looked new, fresher, brighter.

He'd crawled across the burning bridge back to life again. *Thank You, Lord Jesus*.

His arm and shoulder ached and begged for a painkiller. He returned to the couch and the heating pad. As he stretched out again, trembling with fatigue but pleased, too, he heard a car door slam.

Who could that be? He'd told everyone he'd be gone for a full week.

Footsteps sounded on the hollow wooden porch. He lay still. They'd leave when they realized he wasn't home.

Someone knocked. "Quinn, are you there?"

His breath seeped out. Gena. What was she doing here?

The knock sounded again, more insistent. "I know someone is in there. The light is on. Open up before I call the police and report a robbery."

Quinn groaned at his own stupidity. He'd been careful to keep lights out until after Derrick fed the cats and he'd been too sick the first couple of days to turn one on. But Derrick had come and gone, and tonight, feeling better, Quinn had flipped on the kitchen light to heat the broth.

"Hello!" The pounding came again.

There was nothing he could do but stumble to the door and open it.

She was the prettiest sight he'd ever seen. And he wished she'd stayed away. He didn't want her to see him like this.

"Quinn, when did you get back? I tried to call—" As her eyes took him in, she froze. "You're sick. Are you sick?"

She pushed inside the living room. He backed away. "Don't come near. I haven't showered in five days."

"Hush," she said, and led him like a mindless robot to the couch. "You're white as a ghost. Sit down before you collapse."

He collapsed anyway, but the couch caught him.

She sat beside him, her professional hands going through all the motions. She took his pulse, felt his head with her wrist, assessed him with long, intelligent stares.

The pleasure of being cared for melted him. He was mush in her hands.

Go away. But the silent command was as weak as he was.

"What's going on, Quinn? You look like—"

"Roadkill?" He managed a shaky smile.

"Worse. What's wrong?"

He lacked the energy to lie or rummage up a clever response. She was too smart, and he respected her too much for any more lies. "Oxycodone. We battled. I won."

Wisdom shifted behind her eyes. The tumblers lined up.

"Oh." The word came out in a soft breath.

He rocked to a stand, proud that he could, and wobbled the few feet to the cabinet over the sink. He wrapped his fingers around the bottle.

"Here." Pills rattled against plastic as he dropped them into her outstretched palm. "I don't need them anymore."

He *wanted* them, but with God's help, he'd find other ways to control his pain, both mental and physical.

"You detoxed alone? Quinn! That could be dangerous."

"No other choice."

"Your family doesn't know, do they? That's why you've avoided them. That's why you've hidden yourself out here on the river."

He flopped back against the sofa cushions, too weak to sit up any longer.

"A Buchanon with a drug problem?" He shook his head. "Can't happen. I won't bring that shame on my family."

"You're human, Quinn. With the surgeries you've endured and the chronic pain. What happened to you can happen to anyone."

"Not in my family."

"They would understand. They love you."

He shook his head. "Christians don't do drugs."

"Really? And what scientific study told you that? Christians are as human as anyone. Pain. Trouble. Temptation. They come to all of us." She angled toward him, passionate in her speech. "We're not tempted because we're evil. We're tempted because we're human. You've been through a great deal of loss and pain for a long time."

"Don't sympathize with the guilty."

She was silent for a few moments and Quinn closed his eyes, resting. He was bone weary. Dead tired.

"How long?"

He knew what she asked. How long was he dependent? He didn't open his eyes. He didn't want to see her shock when she learned that he had been more than tempted. He was a big-time failure. "Six months. This time."

She touched the top of his hand. "You've been through this before?"

Quinn glanced at her, humiliated, ashamed, remorseful. Why had she come over? Another day and he could have pretended that none of this ever happened.

"After the accident twelve years ago, I spent hours in reconstruction. An infection set in to the bone."

She nodded, too sympathetic, green eyes soft with compassion. "Osteomyelitis pain is off the scale."

Tell him about it. "More surgeries followed. They were fighting to save my arm."

"And your life."

That, too, though there had been times he'd wished they hadn't. "The hospital pumped me full of drugs. I didn't even know what was happening until I started asking for shots and pills I didn't need."

"But you got off them."

"As soon as I realized. Detox was hard but not terrible because I caught the problem right away. This time, I knew better than to let them get me. I promised to only take the painkillers for a couple of weeks during the worst of the post-op pain. But two weeks became three. Every day, I'd vow that tomorrow would be better. The need got worse. I should have seen this coming but I didn't until I was in trouble."

She stared at the bottle. "I would have helped you get through this safely."

"I couldn't ask. I tried."

"I suspected as much that last night at my place. Your behavior was…bizarre." A smile flickered. "Even for you."

"I didn't want anyone to know, especially you."

"You thought I'd pass judgment?"

"Wouldn't you?"

"No! I'm a medical professional."

He raised hot, dry eyes to her green ones. "You're more than that, Gena. A lot more."

Her lips fell open as she absorbed what he was trying to tell her.

"I couldn't start something with you until this was resolved. You deserve better."

"Are we starting something?"

He rolled his head on the cushions but didn't raise himself up. With a shaky laugh, he said, "Not tonight."

She smiled and glanced at her ever-present nurse's watch. "I have to pick up Derrick soon, but I'll leave some instructions. They'll make you feel better."

"Thanks." He licked his dry lips. The roof of his mouth was dry as talc.

"Do you mind if I rummage in your bathroom cabinet?"

"If you can stand being in there."

Apparently, she could, because she left him. He heard water running before she returned with a couple of medicine bottles.

"I'm filling the tub. Get in it. The heat will ease the body aches."

He nodded.

She shook some pills into her palm. "Take these now."

He waved her off. "No drugs."

"Vitamins and ibuprofen. Tomorrow I'll bring some supplements that should help."

"No valium. Nothing but vitamins."

"Are you sure? I can prescribe something to make this easier."

"No drugs. None. Zero." He downed the vitamins and Motrin with Gatorade.

Silent, she studied him before saying, "You're through the worst anyway but I'd be remiss as a practitioner if I didn't discuss some options with you."

"Such as?"

"Narcotics Anonymous meets in Paris every week. You should attend."

"No."

"Addiction is mental as well as physical, Quinn. You're going to want those pills again."

He snorted. "You mean like now?"

"Exactly. You need to work through a program with people who understand what you're going through. They'll assign you a mentor to talk to when you're tempted or when you've had a lousy day."

"Not interested."

"I'll go with you."

That gave him pause. "You would?"

"Absolutely. It's an hour away, Quinn. No one will know."

She understood how desperately he wanted to keep this from his family, and he loved her for it. Loved her for being here. Just plain loved her.

Tonight he was as vulnerable as a baby.

"Someone might recognize me. As arrogant as that

sounds, my picture was in every paper and magazine in this state. I was on TV every week. People in this part of Texas don't forget. I won't go to meetings, Gena."

Those intelligent eyes blinked, calculating. "Then I'll be your NA partner, the person to call if you hit a wall or need a pill or have a problem."

"Nights are the roughest. I don't want to do that to you."

"I'm not asking. I'm telling you. Day or night, call or text and I'll be there to listen and advise. If you don't call me, I'll be ringing your phone or pounding your door at two in the morning. I want you well, Quinn."

"A man could fall madly in love with a woman like you. You know that?"

That he already loved her was beside the point. He was getting clean. But he wasn't there yet. Until then he should keep his mouth shut. "Sorry. I'm not myself tonight."

She gave him a long, contemplative look. "I see that."

His head fell back. He wanted her to stay. He wished she would go.

She went into the bathroom and turned off the water. When she returned, she said, "I'm leaving. Will you be all right?"

"Go."

"For what it's worth, Quinn, I'm proud of you. You're a strong man. Stubborn and reckless, but pretty amazing. Anyone can fall down, even a Christian. Calling on God to get you back up—that's special." She kissed him on the sweaty, stinky forehead, pushing back his dirty hair. "Call me if you need anything. No matter the time. I'll see you in the morning."

She let herself out, for which he would be eternally grateful. He needed the tiny amount of energy he had left to get off this couch and follow her instructions.

Proud?

He didn't think so.

* * *

At a little past eight the next morning, after dropping Derrick at school, Gena tapped at Quinn's door and let herself inside. Apparently, he hadn't bothered to turn the lock after she'd left. She would scold, but he had probably been too weak and fuzzy headed last night to remember.

She still could barely believe he'd gone through the past five days alone. Opiate withdrawal was rarely deadly and patients varied in their reactions, but he'd been in real danger of other complications. He must have known, and yet that stubborn pride of his had put his health in jeopardy.

At midnight he'd texted to say he was all right, which meant he'd been awake. She'd telephoned and they'd talked for fifteen minutes until he yawned. After hanging up, she'd prayed for him, for herself, and had fallen asleep with the prayers on her lips.

"Quinn?" Holding a plastic grocery bag in one hand, she stood inside the cabin door. He wasn't on the couch. "Are you okay?"

A door to the side opened and he came out, a towel around his shoulders. "Morning."

"You look…better." *Better* was a stretch. Hollow eyed with dark circles and sunken cheeks, he remained color- less and the lines of his mouth dug deep grooves.

On the upside, he looked and smelled clean. His golden- brown hair stuck up, wet and shiny. Barefoot, he wore clean pajama flannels and a T-shirt.

"You said that rather dubiously." He sank onto the couch, another sign of malaise. "I'm definitely im- proved. More like I've been hit by a minivan instead of an 18-wheeler."

She was tempted to hug him. Maybe even kiss him. She was that proud of him. Proud and smitten.

Last night he'd said he wanted a relationship with her. Although she'd wondered if his head was clear enough for such declarations, her heart had leaped when he'd said he could love a woman like her.

She wanted that.

But then there was Derrick.

Compartmentalizing her personal thoughts, Gena went into nurse mode. "Did you drink the liquids I prescribed?"

"Yes, Doc."

"Breakfast?"

He grimaced. "Later, maybe."

"I brought cream of wheat, soups, yogurt, ice cream and a nutrition drink. Try those today and gradually work up from there." She walked the few steps into the kitchen and put the bag on the counter. "We'll start with the cream of wheat and milk. Okay?"

"You don't take no for an answer, do you?" He didn't sound excited.

She clanged around in the cabinets until she found a pot and put water on to boil. "How about a cup of sweetened tea with mint. Mint soothes the stomach."

"I can handle that." He produced a comb from somewhere and ran it through his hair. "You don't have to be here, Gena. I got this."

She turned and met his stare. "I want to be."

His hand paused in midcomb. He held her look until her blood hummed with a peculiar sense of happiness.

"You have work."

"I'll get there."

At the appointed two-and-a-half minutes, she poured the steaming cream of wheat into a bowl and sprinkled on a spoon of brown sugar and enough milk to cool it. "At the table or on the sofa?"

"There." Gingerly, he made his way to the table and began to eat. "This is not bad."

"Haven't you ever had cream of wheat?"

"Not that I remember."

"I kept it bland today but you can add other ingredients for extra flavor."

"My stomach thanks you."

Gena pulled a chair up next to him and looked him over.

He gave her a sideways glance. "Stop staring. I feel like a specimen under your microscope."

"You are."

He snorted. "And what do you see?"

The man I want to love.

"Night of the living dead." When he gave her another sideways scowl, she added "…resurrecting."

"Go ahead. Kick a man while he's down."

She patted his forearm. "I'm kidding. You look better than last night. Your prognosis is awesomeness."

The corners of his mouth tilted. He finished the cereal and pushed aside the bowl. "A couple more days and I'll be back to normal. If I can remember what that felt like."

"You will." She glanced at her watch and stood. "I should go."

He caught her wrist. "Skip work. Stay here with me."

Her heart lurched. She wanted to do exactly that. Foolish, foolish heart that had no logic at all. The man was recovering from drug dependency. He was moody and grouchy. He was her nephew's secret father. All perfectly good reasons why she should run like a scared rabbit and never look back.

But he was also caring and tenderhearted, smart and witty. Hadn't he made a difference in Derrick's attitude, shown the boy compassion and support and how to fix a tire and throw a spiral? He was a man with the strength of character to beat a powerful opiate cold turkey, sparing his family the embarrassment and anxiety. Even with his issues, Quinn Buchanon was a man to admire. A man to love.

"Tempting."

Quinn's long fingers curled around hers and tugged her close to his chair. His other arm slid around her waist. He stared up at her, made her heart flutter.

"I thought you were weak." She rested against him, liking it there, but careful of his shoulder.

"Cream of wheat. Breakfast of champions."

"Powerful stuff." She pulled back and he followed her up. She felt him quiver and knew he wasn't as strong as he let on. "You rest today, and I'll bring you a present—a shake from the Tiger's Den after work."

"They make the best." He leaned into her, and she wasn't sure if the move was romantic or survival. She braced her feet and rubbed her hand lightly over his shoulder.

"What's your favorite flavor?" They were as close as a kiss.

"Strawberry." He closed his eyes. "That feels good."

"This?" She gently kneaded his damaged shoulder, moving from trapezius to biceps. Hardened scar tissue knotted beneath her fingertips. "I don't want to hurt you."

"I'm tough."

"You won't get an argument from this nurse, but I want to ease pain, not cause it."

His eyelids lifted to half-mast. "You make me better by being here."

Oh, that was dangerous.

"Exactly the purpose of a mentor." She gave his shoulder one final rub and shifted away. "I have to get to work. Follow the instructions I left on the counter. Eat. Drink. Take those supplements. I'll stop in after the clinic closes."

Quinn made a sound of protest but followed her to the door.

"If you want anything from town, text me."

He touched her cheek, expression tender. "You've thought of everything."

If that was true, she wouldn't be in this dilemma.

Chapter Thirteen

Quinn was a tad on the queasy side for reasons other than drug withdrawal. A week had passed, spring flowered in all her colorful glory and each day, he reclaimed more of his health and his life. In celebration, he'd grilled T-bones for Gena and Derrick last night.

This, however, was the one gauntlet he'd yet to run, the one thing he'd not been able to do since the accident.

Surprising blessing that she'd become, Gena was at his side. She didn't know how difficult this was for him or that he'd not attended a football game of any kind since before the accident.

Tonight, however, was for the twerp as much as to prove to himself that he could be here—in the stands instead of on the field—and not fall into a black hole of depression.

He stepped to the ticket window and put down his money. The woman at the counter counted out his change and looked with speculation between Quinn and the pretty blonde at his side. "Hi, Quinn. Gena. How's it going?"

Better than he deserved. "Great, Shelby. You?"

That wasn't so bad. He sounded natural and if he could get past the knotted belly, he'd admit he'd missed this. The atmosphere was electric and the air ripe with spring and eager, nervous boys and their parents.

The middle school band thundered out an energetic, if somewhat squeaky, GC fight song. Quinn's blood began to hum. He yearned to be out there.

Kids ran up and down the sidelines and a train of people gathered at the wooden concession window, where hot dogs and popcorn scented the air. Gold-and-black crepe paper streamers fluttered from the goalposts and cheerleaders in short skirts sold mini pom-poms to fans.

"What's in the box?" the ticket taker asked, drawing him out of his reverie.

Gena perched the cardboard container on one hip and lifted out a kitten. "Quinn has two kittens to give away."

The other woman laughed and pushed out with both hands. "Smart to bring them here, but I don't want one. Some kid will nag his parents into taking one."

"That's the plan."

Solid-black Optimus now made his home with Derrick and the cuddly white kitten had charmed Charity, leaving the two tuxedos. Tonight he'd be finished with cats. He glanced at a sweet black-and-white face and gave her a pat. He wasn't a cat person. She had to go.

Quinn retrieved the box from Gena, and they made their way to the stands, stopping to chat, to let people coo over the kittens and to discuss the merits of the GC Tigers against the Sanderville Bears. Even a middle school scrimmage brought the town together.

"I told the coach I'd sit near the bottom in case someone needed attention," Gena said.

"Whatever you say, Doc." They landed on the second bleacher and set the box next to them. At seven weeks, they were ready for adoption, but regardless of his protest to the contrary, he'd miss the little fur balls.

"It's been a long time," he said, gazing out over the field.

"Has it?"

She felt so right sitting next to him in black scrubs and a

black GC sweatshirt with her blond hair down around her shoulders and her side brushing his. A good woman who forgave his shortcomings and treated him like someone special, Gena Satterfield was the special one.

"First time since the accident."

"Really?" She angled her face toward him. Beautiful woman. "Why?"

He shrugged. "Good question."

"Will it bother you to be here? I didn't think of that when Derrick cornered you."

"Derrick is the point. This isn't about me."

She slid her hand down the sleeve of his jacket and joined her fingers with his. "He tried to play nonchalant, but he's very excited that you're here. The other boys have suddenly decided he's cool, thanks to you."

"Not me. Derrick's a decent kid. The others just had to open their eyes and give him a chance."

"Still." Her smile took his breath. "Thank you."

"For that smile, I'd run out on the field and do a pom routine."

She laughed. "I'd love to see that."

He warmed her hand with his and held her snuggled against his side. The cool evening air made his arm ache but with her near, the pain didn't matter as much.

After the national anthem, the game began with a burst of gold-and-black-clad boys racing onto the field to meet the red-and-white Bears. Derrick stood on the sidelines, helmet in hand, with the other sixth graders.

"Do you think he'll get to play?" Gena asked.

"It's a scrimmage. They'll all get in a few minutes."

"I'm nervous."

Quinn snorted. So was he but he wasn't saying so. "The twerp will do great."

"But his psyche is so fragile. If anything goes wrong…"

He squeezed her hand. "In football, things always go wrong. It's part of the game. He knows that. Relax."

In minutes, two little girls, probably eight or nine, stopped in front of Gena. "Hi, Miss Gena. Clayton said you have baby kittens."

That was the fame of Gena. Everyone in town seemed to know the kind and friendly nurse practitioner. How had he missed out on her for so long?

He knew the answer, loathed it, but now that he'd fought the darkness and won, he planned to make up for lost time. He'd seen her every day last week and all day Sunday. And still, the hours together weren't enough. She was an oasis to a dry, thirsty man.

"Would you like to pet one?" Gena was saying to the girls.

Two eager faces bobbed up and down.

Gena extracted her hand from his. He scowled at the loss, and she chuckled. "Kittens are kid magnets."

"Do you know how to hold a cat?" Quinn asked. "They're babies. You can hurt them."

He must have sounded gruffer than he'd intended because two pairs of eyes widened.

"Quinn," Gena rebuked mildly. "They're fine."

She handed a kitten to each girl. The sweet felines, thanks to Derrick's gentle care, snuggled and purred, bringing oohs and giggles from the girls.

Miss Brown Ponytail said, "Can I go ask my mama if I can have one?"

"Absolutely, Amy."

Leave it to Gena to know their names.

"Me, too, Miss Gena. My daddy's right up there." The other little face puckered in a frown. "He hates cats."

"Me, too," Quinn said and received a pair of hopeful looks.

"Can I show him this one? I think I'll call him Fluffy."

When the two girls clambered up the steps, each with a kitten across her shoulder, Quinn frowned at Gena. "What kind of name is Fluffy for a male cat?"

"Subject to change, I hope. But I'm starting to think you don't want to give them away."

"Sure I do. But they deserve good homes, not places that call them sissy names. Strips a guy's manhood. Can you imagine if my mom had named me Fluffy?"

She snorted. "Little girls make great kitten owners, and both Amy and Chelsea are kind children with good parents. If they take one each, rejoice!"

"I suppose. Now, get back over here beside me. I can't romance you with a couple of cats between us." He tugged her hand. She scooted close again and peace settled over him.

"There's your sister."

Charity, with her young daughter toting a hot dog and Coke, climbed the steps onto the bleachers. One of his brothers, Sawyer, loomed behind her. Every female eye in the stadium followed the movie-star handsome man exuding confidence and male charisma. With a fierce stir of possessiveness, he glanced at Gena. Her eyes twinkled his way as if she could read his thoughts.

Dangerous woman. Incredible, smart woman he was falling in love with. The problem was, each time he advanced, she retreated, but when he retreated, she advanced. A mating dance, he supposed, even though he wondered what her problem was. She liked him. He was certain. Maybe she held last week's event against him. Maybe she feared he'd fall again.

The possibility was there. He'd succumbed before, but with God's help, Gena's support and his own fiercely determined will, he wouldn't. Still, she had a right to hold him at arm's length until he proved himself worthy. Distance didn't stop him from wanting her.

Charity spotted him and motioned to Sawyer. Like a flock of pretty blackbirds, they descended, and in seconds he was surrounded by family. It felt good.

Sawyer sat on one side of him. Charity and her seven-year-old daughter, Amber, took Gena's side, and the women chatted about Derrick and Ryan, the kitten and town events he wasn't involved in. He needed to change that.

"Hey, bro, good job." Sawyer gently poked a fist against his left shoulder.

Quinn cocked an eyebrow. "Meaning?"

The twin hitched his head toward Gena. "Love is in the air."

He hoped so. "She could have any guy in town."

"She's here with you, isn't she? Confess. The two of you are seeing each other. And I do mean *seeing* as in kissy-kissy. The fam thinks she might be the one."

He was thinking the same thing. "They're talking about us?"

"Wondering if you'll get your head out of the sand and step up to the plate. Grab the bull by the horns, so to speak."

Quinn screwed up his face on purpose. "Do you know how little sense that made?"

"Will you or won't you? I'm your brother. You can talk to me."

"Maybe." Until he was sure he was more than a patient under Gena's protective eye, he wasn't ready to share with his mouthy family.

"You should be in politics." Sawyer pointed to the field. "Number sixty-four is a hoss. Did you see him tackle?"

Quinn focused on the field for a moment. Though he'd love to be out there in the thick of the game, he was doing okay. Better than he'd thought. Being here felt pretty okay.

After a field goal by the opposing team, Sawyer groaned

and slapped his knee. "Their offensive line is ransacking our defense."

"Speaking of ransacking," Quinn said, "any news from the sheriff on the vandalism at the Huckleberry Addition?"

"He thinks it's the same person. Otherwise, he's as clueless as we are."

"From the note Brady found back at Christmas, the acts appear personal, as though one of us has made someone really angry."

"You made fools of plenty of football opponents."

"Nah. Whoever is sabotaging Buchanon Built projects is focused on the company, not an individual."

"You sure about that?"

Frustrated, Quinn said, "No."

Suddenly, Gena grabbed his arm and squeezed hard. "Quinn. Derrick is going in."

He turned his attention to the field and number sixteen, long and lanky, trotting onto the field to the quarterback position.

The first play was a handoff to the running back, who scampered for a couple of yards. The third play resulted in a sack. Derrick went down under a pile of bodies. Gena sucked in half the air in the stadium and stood up. Quinn was right beside her.

"A sack is part of the game. He's all right."

She nodded but didn't breathe again until Derrick popped up, slapped a teammate on the head and jogged back to the huddle.

"See? He's up." They both sat again, and Quinn was more relieved that he wanted to let on. The kid was new at this. He was only eleven. The linebacker who'd snagged him was huge, probably eighth grade, at least. "He'll make them pay for that. Just wait."

After a sack, success was a quarterback's best revenge.

On third down and long yardage, Derrick danced backward from the line of bodies.

Quinn leaped to his feet, bringing the crowd with him. "That a boy. Do it. Do it."

Gena gripped his arm until the blood flow nearly stopped.

Receivers scattered downfield to the right and left.

Quinn saw everything with a clarity that stunned him. Even after all this time, he read the defense and knew what was about to happen. He saw the blocks off the line and the big boys up front protecting the sixth-grade quarterback. He spotted the open receiver.

"Not him, Derrick," he muttered. "The safety's too close."

Derrick danced for long, unnerving seconds before firing the ball exactly where Quinn would have. To the tight end on a crossing route. As if in slow motion, the prettiest spiral imaginable sailed in an arc and slammed into the receiver's hands.

A cheer erupted, none louder than Gena's high-pitched ear splitter. She whirled toward Quinn, who was grinning like a maniac.

"He did it! He did it!" She leaped into his arms, hopping and squealing and pounding his chest with her palm. "Did you see him?"

He laughed down at her, adoring her and so happy for the twerp he kissed her, at first with a short smack that felt so warm and soft and good that he went back for more. Long and sweet enough that the crowd noise sort of faded. Then Sawyer elbowed him.

He pulled away, laughing, delighted with her and this incredible emotion she bubbled up in him, and for the boy who even now searched the stands, helmet at his side, eager faced and grinning.

One arm around a smiling Gena, Quinn lifted his opposite hand in a pumped fist. Derrick waved his helmet and jogged off the field.

He and Gena slapped high fives and grinned at each other in pride.

It was almost as if they were the kid's real parents.

After the game, he'd taken them out for pizza. The whole team. While the boys ravaged through pizza as fast as the Tiger's Den could bake, Quinn and she sat in a quieter corner talking. About the game. The lone female kitten that hadn't found a home. About everything and anything.

Her reclusive, cranky neighbor was turning into a sociable guy. Gena had been falling for the first Quinn. She was head over heels for the new one.

She was walking a tightrope without a safety net. And she was doomed for a fall.

These thoughts had plagued her every time she had a free moment at the clinic. Thankfully, free moments didn't come often.

Yet here she was again spending all day Saturday at Quinn's cabin as if she couldn't stay away, as if he held some kind of magnetic force field that drew her across the woods and fields to him.

Derrick sprawled on the living room floor with the remaining kitten curled on his chest. Derrick hadn't asked if he could bring the cat in. He'd simply said in an accusing tone, "She's crying out there by herself."

Quinn had growled and scowled but the cat was still inside.

"You're a teddy bear," she said, bumping his side as they washed dishes from lunch.

He flipped water on her.

She dodged, laughed and flapped the tea towel in a wimpy whack. "Derrick said you came to all the practices last week."

"Stopped by. Coach asked me to stick around and work with the quarterbacks and receivers." He shook his head. "I never thought of myself as a coach."

She saw the light in his expression. "You enjoy it."

"Surprisingly." He rinsed the last dish and pulled the drain plug.

"Will you continue?"

"Richardson asked if I was interested."

"You should do it, Quinn. You love football."

"Loved."

"Still do. You took a hiatus and went on injured reserve. Isn't that what they call it?"

"Listen to you. Football lingo."

"Seriously. The boys look up to you. You'd be a great role model and a lot of help to the kids and the coach."

"Role model? Me?"

"Yes, you. Deal with it."

He dried his hands on the end of her towel, and she could see he was thinking some serious thoughts.

Derrick pushed off the floor and ambled into the kitchen space. "The guys like it when you're at practice, Quinn. They get fired up."

"Everybody tries to impress him?" Gena asked with a smile.

"Pretty much. He's old, but he's all right, I guess."

Eyes sparking with humor and challenge, Quinn grunted and hooked an elbow around Derrick's neck. "I can still take you on, twerp."

"Ha. Prove it."

"I think I heard a challenge, Quinn." Gena hung the tea towel over the oven bar.

"I'm up for a game." He glanced her way. "Are you?"

"Me?" she asked.

"No," he said sarcastically, "the other gorgeous blonde in my kitchen."

"Wise guy," she said, but was buoyed by the sweet words. True or not, he made her feel beautiful in a way no one ever had. She actually believed him. Her. Geeky, nerdy, egghead Gena felt pretty.

"Gena's on my team." Derrick danced around on the balls of his feet like a prizefighter in the ring. From somewhere, he'd produced a football and he slapped it back and forth in his hands.

"Oh-ho! Ganging up on me, eh?" Quinn patted Derrick's head. "Doesn't matter. Two, three or five of you, prepare to be decimated by a master."

With a loud hoot, Derrick raced for the door but paused in the living room to scoop the kitten off Quinn's throw blanket. "She can watch from the porch."

The adults followed the enthused boy out into the yard and the silliest, rowdiest game of football ever played commenced. Gena laughed so much she was forced to the sidelines of their pretend football field to hold her side and catch her breath.

Meanwhile, Derrick weaved in and around Quinn with the football, laughing, taunting as only a sixth grader can do and mocking the much larger man. When Quinn caught him around the waist with a powerful left arm and swirled him gingerly to the ground, the boy lay flat on his back cradling the football and staring up at the sky with the happiest grin she had seen in nearly two years.

"I give," he said.

Quinn offered a hand up. Derrick popped up like a jackrabbit, agile and light on his feet. The two males stood panting, hands on their hips, eyeballing each other. Grinning.

Two peas in a pod. Didn't they see it? Or was she so terribly paranoid she imagined the similarities?

Quinn clapped the boy on the back and said, "Good try, twerp."

As Quinn turned his back, an idea hit Gena. Motioning frantically until she caught her nephew's eye, she held her hands up. Derrick fired a pass. Amazingly, she caught it and scampered into the pretend end zone.

"Touchdown!" Derrick shot both arms into the air and raced to Gena for a leaping double high five.

Quinn whirled back around, expression incredulous. "You didn't…?"

"We did." Gena danced toward him. "And we win, big guy. The girl and the kid win! Face it. You've been skunked. Outsmarted."

"Outscored." Derrick strutted around cocky as a rooster and flipped the ball to Quinn. "Admit it, dude. I'm the man. Gena's the wo-man."

Quinn groaned and slapped the ball. "I'm done. You got me."

Derrick preened, but suspicion sprouted in Gena. "You're giving up that easily? The Mighty Quinn?"

He hung his head, looking pitiful, and just when she believed him, he yelled, "No!" and raced toward the other goal.

"Hey!" Gena and Derrick rushed after him, but the surprise attack and head start gave Quinn the advantage. Just as he crossed the goal line, Gena cried, "Get him!"

In an athletic move she didn't know she had, Gena dove into his chest while Derrick went for the legs. The Mighty Quinn came down with an *oomph*.

Breathless and laughing, they all three sprawled flat on their backs on the grass like the aftermath of destruction.

She couldn't remember feeling this happy in a long time. She rolled her head toward the man flopped an arm's length away. When she'd moved to Gabriel's Crossing, her life had been Derrick and her career and little else. Meeting a certain cranky neighbor had changed that.

Derrick sat up and dusted the grass and dirt from his

T-shirt. Relaxed, expression content, he said to Quinn, "You're not so bad for an old guy."

"You're not so bad for a little twerp."

Apparently, the male banter delighted them both. Quinn hopped to his feet and reached down a hand for Gena. "Ma'am."

"Don't do anything tricky," she said cautiously as she placed a hand in his. "The game is over."

"Would I do that?" he asked innocently.

"Yes, you would."

"Because you cheated, you think I'd take revenge?"

She tilted her head in a shrug. "Maybe."

He tugged her gently to her feet but instead of letting go, he gave one hard yank and she landed in his arms.

"You cheat," he whispered. "But I like you." Then he kissed her.

"Oh, please." Derrick coughed and rolled his eyes. "I'm dying over here."

"You'll understand someday," Quinn growled, but turned her loose and retrieved the ball from the ground.

He tossed the football to Derrick. The boy one-handed it without his usual cocky grin.

Fingering the laces, eyes down, Derrick spoke in a low, yearning voice. "I wish I had a dad, especially if he was cool like you."

Gena's heart fell. Her fantasy world came crashing down.

Derrick needed a dad, and Quinn deserved to know, even though she feared his reaction. He wouldn't be happy that she'd kept the truth from him. But she didn't quite believe any longer that he'd take Derrick away from her.

Though rough around the edges and socially rusty, he was a decent man with a wonderful family. Derrick needed that.

Everything in her wanted to blurt the truth.

Everything except a vow she'd made before God.

Chapter Fourteen

Long after Gena and Derrick went home, Quinn thought about Derrick's heart-touching comment. For a tough kid who pretended not to care, he had an ache inside him that beat any ache Quinn's arm had ever suffered.

The idea of him—Quinn Buchanon—being a cool dad was laughable. Wasn't it? Not that he would mind being a father, but the subject had never come up. Not back in the day when he'd dated through a half-dozen sororities. Then when his world collapsed, he'd considered himself lousy husband and father material. But now with Gena as the mom—yes, he could see that. Funny how the right woman could make a man look at the world differently.

"What do you think, girl?"

Sitting on the porch stoop, he picked up the lone kitten. She was still a tiny thing that fit in his palm. She blinked up with her mother's bright yellow eyes. When he ran a finger over the top of her head, she snuggled into his hand, purring and nudging for more.

"Don't try to talk me into anything. I'm not the cat-loving kind. I won't fall for it. Just ask your mother."

Yeah, and if he'd let the lady cat in the house, maybe she'd still be around for her babies.

He settled the kitten on his lap and watched her. "You're

a pretty girl. How do you feel about mice? Could you catch one?"

She curled into a fuzzy comma and closed her eyes.

"That's what I figured. A diva."

His cell phone sounded from somewhere. The kitten perked up, back arched and ears erect as she sought the evil noise.

Quinn laughed. "Ninja cat?"

He stroked a hand over her high back, and she forgot about the ringing phone.

Listening, too lazy and content from the afternoon with Gena to get up and not really caring to have his Saturday off interrupted, he pinpointed the phone's general location. How had it gotten out there?

"I need a secretary, not a cat."

The kitten hopped down and followed the noise. Eventually, the ringing stopped.

When the kitten looked back over one shoulder as if to say, "Are you coming or not?" Quinn got up.

"Demanding diva. Just what I need."

He followed her to the shed, where he found his cell phone in the kitten's padded box.

"Don't ask me," he said as he punched in the voice mail, listened with a deepening frown at his father's aggravated voice then pressed Redial.

"Dad. What's up?"

"Trouble on the Hammonds' house."

He groaned. "Not again."

"Bigger. Worse."

"Than a fire?"

"No, not that bad, thank the Lord. I need all you boys on the site ASAP."

Quinn sighed. So much for his pleasant Saturday. "On my way."

After securing the kitten, he drove to the Huckleberry

Addition and into the cul-de-sac. A series of beautiful Buchanon Built homes in various stages of completion sat on roomy lots surrounded by the right number of undisturbed trees. When completed, this addition would be a great place to live. If they ever got it completed.

Today the place crawled with trucks and people, mostly Buchanons. Brady, Dawson, Sawyer and Dad. Even his mom and Charity were on the site. Leroy, a police officer who was also a good friend of the family, talked to a befuddled man in a denim ball cap. Quinn recognized the subcontractor, Mack Wyman, a man who handled the Buchanon Built dirt work, driveway building, sod application and a host of other necessary big-equipment jobs.

This couldn't be good.

Quinn parked along the edge of the street and loped to the gathered group.

"What's happened?"

The subcontractor removed his ball cap and scratched his head. "I had a Bobcat parked out back."

"The skid steer?" Quinn nodded. "I saw it yesterday."

The police officer stepped up. "Then you're the last person to have seen it on site."

"You mean the Bobcat's gone? A piece of equipment that big?"

"Whoever took it knew what they were doing. They didn't load it. They drove it. You can see the tracks."

"Unbelievable." Quinn rubbed his jaw. "The only occupied houses are a block down the street but someone must have noticed a big yellow machine coming past."

Officer Leroy's head bobbed. "I'll canvass the area and find out."

Grimly, Dawson motioned to the house. "They paid us a visit before they stole the Bobcat."

Quinn tipped his head back, looking up but not really seeing the faded blue sky. "Not again."

"Same old, same old. Busted walls. Paint dumped on the new carpet."

A sick feeling rose in Quinn's throat. "This house was almost completed."

Sawyer nodded. "All we lacked was Mack's yard work, final inspections and touch-ups."

"Might as well grab a clipboard and assess repairs," Dan said. "This house is sold. We'll have to get started on cleanup first thing in the morning."

"Not tomorrow," Quinn said. "Sorry, Dad. Church and family day."

His three brothers turned to stare at him.

"Church? Again?"

"So?" Quinn said. "What of it?"

"Who are you?" Brody asked, eyes wide. "And what have you done with my reclusive, grouchy brother?"

"I know what happened," Sawyer said with a sage nod and speculative gleam in his eyes. "Gena Satterfield, most lovely nurse and delightful neighbor."

Quinn deepened his scowl. Sawyer was right, at least in part. He wanted to be with Gena, but he wanted to be with his family again, too. Most of all, God deserved his time and thanks and he planned to give it. He'd played the prodigal long enough.

His father surprised him with a pat on the back. "Whatever the reason, your mother and I are glad. She's cried and prayed for you more than any of her kids."

"Thanks, Dad. Way to make a man feel like a jerk."

Brady laughed. "If the shoe fits—"

"Okay, okay. Lay off." They didn't know and he would never tell them, but Mom's prayers had kept him going. Now that he was clean, he wanted back in the fold.

"If you're not working tomorrow, we're losing daylight today," Dad said. "The place won't get clean by itself."

With a frustrated sigh, Quinn headed into the house. Was this vandalism ever going to stop?

Gena's feet were propped on the distressed coffee table, a retro piece she'd found in the attic that suited her taste. She and Renae had played tea party on this table. They'd also done exactly what she was doing now. Polishing her toenails.

"I miss you, sis," she said, and Derrick's kitten, curled on a throw pillow at her elbow, opened a sleepy eye. When he realized she was not offering a snack, Optimus dozed again.

The afternoon with Quinn had been such fun until Derrick's unintentionally dangerous remark. She was stumped. There was no good solution. If she told Quinn, she betrayed Renae. If she didn't tell him, she'd be stuck in limbo forever. Whatever relationship they had couldn't advance, not with a lie between them.

He'd come clean with her about the pills.

But that was different, wasn't it? Derrick wasn't her secret. He was Renae's, and her sister wasn't here to make the decision.

With hands steady enough to sew intricate stitches in human flesh, she stroked tiger orange onto her pinkie nail. Her toes were stretched apart with a foam divider.

An engine rumble caught her attention. She recognized the sound. Quinn's big pickup truck.

Her pulse sparked.

In seconds the engine died and he was hammering at her door.

"Come in!" she yelled.

The door opened and he barged in, hands on hips and a scowl that would have scared the average person.

"Why is your door unlocked? And why didn't you ask who was there?"

"I knew it was you," she said mildly. "I am not getting up until my nails dry."

He loomed over her, big and handsome, and she laughed up at him. "You look so fierce."

"Your nails are orange."

"Like them?" She lifted a foot for inspection. "When this dries, I'll paint black tiger stripes."

The light dawned. "Number one Tigers fan?"

"I am now." She sat back but the toes stayed propped. "I didn't expect to see you until tomorrow."

"Vandals destroyed another house."

"Oh, Quinn. I am so sorry. What in the name of all that's good is going on with that?"

"I wish we knew." He lifted the kitten, pillow and all, and sat next to Gena on the couch, repositioning Optimus on his lap.

Gena enjoyed watching the big man soften, watching the kittens and Derrick and the other boys tenderize the hard outer shell he'd been encased in for too long.

"Anything I can do to help?"

"Cheer me up."

"You got it. Want me to sing? Give you a Snoopy Band-Aid and a lollipop? Or beat you in football...again?"

His mouth jerked. "Smart aleck. Speaking of which, where's the twerp?"

"Charity picked him up. She's taking some of the football boys to the movies."

"My big sis. She says he's a model kid when he's with her."

Gena rolled her eyes. "At home he's not quite there yet, but I see progress. His grades are up. He's still mouthy and moody but he's helping around the house more, and he hasn't been in trouble at school in a while."

Since Renae's birthday, as a matter of fact, when he'd opened up to Quinn.

"And apparently, he's making friends."

"Exactly. I've been terrified he'd run away to his scary Houston friends or do something else crazy."

"He's not that bad."

"He was, Quinn." She bit her bottom lip. "In Houston he was arrested for shoplifting. Twice. Both occasions, he was with his gangy friends. It was only a matter of time before they sucked him into drugs and crime."

He huffed out a breath. "Scary business."

"Terrifying. And I'm still learning to be a parent, so knowing the right responses has been doubly difficult."

"You're doing great. He's fortunate to have you in his corner."

"You didn't always think that."

Quinn tilted his head to one side, almost in apology. "A man can change his mind."

"So can a woman." She patted his cheek. "I thought you were the ogre of Texas."

He snorted. "I wasn't too friendly that first meeting, was I?"

"That's putting it mildly." He had no idea that she had arrived with a negative opinion fully formed. Meeting the harsh, threatening neighbor had confirmed the things Renae said about him.

Except she and her sister had both been wrong. Gena didn't know what had happened between Renae and Quinn, but she was wise enough to think there had to be more to the story.

Either that or she was too blinded by love to believe anything bad about Quinn Buchanon.

The problem was, she couldn't ask without raising suspicion.

Quinn leaned close. "You. Me. We are A-L-O-N-E."

"Come to think of it…we are." She corkscrewed her body toward him, careful of her propped toenails.

This close, she noticed the green flecks in his eyes and the lines pain always etched on his handsome face. Flooded with tenderness, she smoothed her fingers along his jaw.

"Your arm is hurting," she said.

"Not bad." He captured her fingers and brought them to his lips, gaze holding hers.

She shivered with the delicious feeling.

He tugged her nearer until she leaned against his side, the pillow and kitten between them like a shield to protect her troubled heart.

Careful not to increase his pain, she rested her head on his shoulder. As if she was fragile, he wrapped her tenderly, carefully, in his arms. She loved feeling cared for and protected, comforted by this man who'd found little comfort of his own.

"You smell good," he murmured against her ear. "Like lemons and spice and everything nice."

She sighed. If the voice in her head would go away, she could be content and happy right here forever.

But the voice nagged worse than a headache.

He deserved to know. She couldn't tell him. A promise was a vow that could not be broken. *Don't forget your sister. But you love Quinn.*

Inwardly, she groaned.

Quinn must have sensed her turmoil. He pulled back. "Something wrong?"

As long as the secret hung between them, being with Quinn wouldn't feel right. She'd let herself grow too close, care too much, and now she had to figure out what to do.

She leaned away, turning to look at her feet as if a pedicure was more important than the incredible man at her side.

"Gena? Are you okay? Did I do something?"

"Could I ask you a question?"

"Anything." He was serious now, anxious, if the grooves in his forehead were any indication.

"You dated my sister."

"A long time ago. Does that matter to you?"

More than he could possibly guess.

She shrugged. "I wondered."

"Wondered what? Renae and I were kids, Gena. College students who lived by the speed-dating rule."

Shocked, she glared. "Are you saying easy come, easy go?"

"I'm saying she dated other guys. I dated other girls."

"So she meant nothing to you. She was only another girl the Mighty Quinn dated."

"I didn't say that. Renae was…special, but after my accident, we went our separate ways."

"I see."

Would they have separated if Quinn had known about Derrick? Had Renae made a mistake by not telling him?

Her bitter sister had branded Quinn an uncaring lout, a playboy with a different girl every weekend.

If he had been, he'd changed. She believed that with all her heart.

Tell him.

But breaking a vow is wrong.

Her thoughts swirled in argument. Could she live with herself if she betrayed Renae?

Could she live with herself if she didn't tell him?

Lord, what am I to do? What's the right thing?

Her heart beat so loud in her chest, she thought Quinn could hear it. Maybe God had opened the door for her to tell him. They were alone. The subject hung between them like a thin veil of trouble.

Sucking in half the air in the room, she studied her shiny orange toenails. "Remember what Derrick said this afternoon?"

"About?"

She glanced sideways at him. "About wishing he had a cool dad?"

"Yeah." He thumped a fist against his chest. "Got me right here."

"Me, too. I feel bad for him. All he has is me and his grandparents in Houston."

"His father's never been in the picture at all?"

"No."

"Must have been a real jerk."

Tell him now. The door is open. Tell him.

He deserved to know. Derrick deserved a father he admired.

Forgive me, Renae.

She opened her mouth to say the words that would change all their lives forever.

The front door slammed back and a pack of preadolescent males rumbled into the living room.

Chapter Fifteen

Early Sunday morning, Gena left a message on Quinn's cell phone.

"Sorry about today. Enjoy church and tell your family hello. Derrick and I are headed to Houston to see my parents. Talk to you soon."

That she'd intended to spend Sunday and the Monday holiday with him was beside the point. Worried she was too in love with Quinn to keep quiet now that God had clearly closed the door on confession, she needed to get away, to think and to talk to her mother. No one understood the situation better than Mom.

She'd nearly opened her mouth and created a disaster.

Derrick slumped in the corner of the passenger seat with earphones in his lap. "I wanted to hang out with Ryan today."

"We haven't seen Grandma and Grandpa in two months."

He gave her the "you're stupid" look she hadn't seen in a while. "Your fault, not mine."

"Derrick," she warned. "Don't start with me."

He jammed the earphones in his ears and crossed his arms, effectively shutting her out.

He didn't know, couldn't ever know that she was running away, at least for a couple of days until she could clear her head.

By the time they reached Houston, Derrick was snoring against the passenger window and Gena's neck and shoulders were in knots. Her parents' hot tub, something she didn't have in Gabriel's Crossing, would feel amazing.

Her parents must have been looking out the window, because they came running the moment Gena killed the Xterra engine. Mom, her artificially blond hair in a short bob, looked the same as always in khaki slacks and a green golf shirt, but the gray in Dad's hair was taking over the brown.

Gena gently shook Derrick's shoulder. He sat up, blurry eyed, and looked around.

"We're here already?"

Her four hours had been longer than his. "Already. There's Grandma and Grandpa."

He hopped out of the car and pretended not to enjoy the hugs and kisses, but he clearly did. He scuffed his tennis shoes, his cheeks pink, and grinned.

Gena's heart squeezed with love. Sometimes he was still very much a little boy.

After lunch, they spent the afternoon catching up. Derrick told his grandparents about football, although they already knew from phone calls, and eventually, Derrick and Grandpa retired to the den to watch the Texas Rangers play the Dodgers.

When the TV noise seeped into the living room, Gena seized the opportunity. "We need to talk in private."

"I figured as much. Come on back to the office. I talk better with something in my hands."

From the hall closet, she withdrew a plastic bin of paints, brushes and a pair of canvases and toted them into the bedroom turned office and craft room.

Painting was one of the crafts Mom and Renae had enjoyed together. "You know I never found my artistic side."

"Oh, try." Mom pushed a paintbrush can at her. "Creating relaxes a person, and you're tense as a fiddle string. Do something simple. It doesn't have to be perfect. Squiggles, a rainbow or whatever comes to you."

"Gallbladders and poison ivy?"

Shaking her head, Mom laughed. "Your choice."

Grinning, Gena took the brush and dipped it into a jar of orange and swirled it in circles on the canvas. "I'm so talented."

"You certainly are. Now, what's going on? Is there a problem with Derrick?"

"Yes and no. As I told you on the phone, he's settling in. The problem isn't directly Derrick. It's more…indirect."

A frown creased her mom's brow. She tilted her head as if examining the tree she'd mysteriously transferred from her hand to the canvas. "I don't follow."

"Renae."

"Oh, honey, we miss her, too."

"Yes, and Derrick still grieves badly, but our grief isn't what I want to discuss."

"Okaaay." Mom applied a few brushstrokes and a forest floor of golden leaves began to appear.

Gena changed brushes. Maybe add some light blue. Like Renae's eyes. "I don't know how to say this except straight-out. I'm amazed Derrick hasn't mentioned him during your phone conversations."

"My grandson is not yet a great conversationalist. I talk and ask questions. He grunts or says, 'Yeah.'"

"That's our Derrick."

"Tell me the problem."

"Quinn Buchanon." There. She'd said the despised name. Reaching for the red paintbrush, Gena braced for the explosion.

Mom glanced over one shoulder as if she worried someone else would hear. In a low, whispery voice, she asked, "What about him?"

"He's my neighbor. I didn't know that when I moved in, but Derrick and I have gotten to know him."

"Do you think that's wise?"

"I don't know." With a frustrated huff, she shoved the brush back into the container. "I like him, Mom, and he connects with Derrick in a way none of us have been able to. He's a good influence."

"I find that hard to believe."

"But, in his own gruff, male way, he is." She shared a few details about their acquaintance, leaving out the fact that she was in love with him.

Mom's brush colored the canvas with short, choppy strokes. "Oh, Gena. I don't know about this. Maybe you and Derrick need to come home."

"We are home. I'm happy in Gabriel's Crossing in a way I never was here. My practice is thriving and Derrick improves every day, and a great deal of the credit for the improvement belongs to Quinn. He is not the man Renae described to us."

"You were there, Gena. You saw what your sister went through because of him."

Gena reached for the yellow brush and drew more swirls on the canvas.

"I want to tell him."

"About Derrick?" Mom held her brush aloft. "No. Honey, you can't. You promised."

"What if Renae's bitterness against Quinn is the wrong thing for Derrick?" *The wrong thing for me?* "Quinn was her personal vendetta, not mine."

"Vendetta? There is nothing vindictive in keeping silent for Derrick's sake. Renae's only concern was for her son."

"Was it? Or did she want to keep on hurting Quinn the way she thought he hurt her?"

"He *did* hurt her. You know that."

"Quinn wasn't the only guy she dated."

"Are you suggesting he isn't Derrick's father?"

"No! Mom, please, you're putting words in my mouth. I'm already confused enough about this. I need your wisdom."

"Has Derrick ever asked about his father?"

"Of course he has. Many times."

"What do you tell him?"

"I sidestep as much as I can, but Derrick can be adamant."

"And?"

"I feed him the story we all agreed upon. Renae never told us." Frustrated, she jabbed a brush into the dark green. "We lie, Mom. Even if we justify it by saying we lie for Derrick's good, a lie is still a lie. I'm terrified of Derrick's reaction if he ever discovers the truth on his own. What happens to our credibility? To the trust?"

"Today our Sunday-school lesson was in Joshua. He was tricked into making a promise to an enemy, but even when he realized his mistake, he kept the promise, and God honored him for it."

"Are you saying the end justifies the means?" *And what about the fact that I'm in love? Doesn't that count for anything?*

"We have to protect Derrick, no matter the cost. You promised. We all did." Tears pooled in her mother's blue eyes. "Keeping Derrick safe from Quinn Buchanon was her dying wish."

Gena glanced away from her mother's sorrowful face. She hadn't come to cause more heartache.

A promise was a promise even if it was a lie. How could that be right?

She stared at her canvas. Gena's painting, like her insides, was a tangled mess.

* * *

Monday holidays meant business to Buchanon Built and all hands on deck. This morning included a team huddle in the office warehouse and a long conversation about the ongoing vandalism.

Quinn had arrived early, moody enough to drink two cups of coffee before the others arrived so he wouldn't bite their heads off.

Gena had stood him up yesterday. He didn't know what was going on, but he missed her. He'd texted her. She'd texted back, asking if he was okay. He wasn't, but not in the way she'd meant.

He poured his third cup and scraped a chair up beside Brady.

"Our visitor left another calling card." Dan spoke from his place at the head of the conference table, a pair of seven-foot folding tables scattered with coffee cups and doughnut boxes.

"Such as?" Quinn reached for a maple doughnut.

His sister Jaylee, queen of health foods and sleek as a cougar, glared at him. "Diabetes in a doughnut."

He flashed his teeth at her and bit down. "Yum."

Brady lofted a plastic bag. "I was at the house last night and found this."

"What is it?"

"A photo." He sailed the bag toward the twins sitting on the opposite side. "Looks like Dawson."

"Me?" Dawson reached for the bag. After a frowning study, he offered the photo to Sawyer.

"Could be either of us," Sawyer said.

"Read the back."

Sawyer turned the picture over. Heads together, he and Dawson looked so much alike only the family noticed the differences. Mirror twins, Sawyer was a dimpleless lefty, while Dawson bore a single dimple in his right cheek.

"'Dawson should have listened,'" he read. "What does that mean?"

"Anyone's guess," Brady said, "but it's the first clue indicating a specific Buchanon rather than the whole family or the company."

"Hurray for me." Dawson made a face.

"We've waited on the police department for too long," Dan said. "The insurance investigator is on my back for more security."

Quinn set down his coffee cup. "Whoever is doing this has disabled every camera and alarm we've erected and seems to know when the houses are empty and no one is around."

"Right," Sawyer added, "and our security guard is only one man. He can't cover every Buchanon building project."

"We could hire more guards."

Dan shook his head. "Not cost-effective. I'm thinking private detective."

"To do what?"

"Pry into Dawson's past and see who he's ticked off."

"Hey!" Dawson dropped his doughnut.

Quinn curled his lip in disagreement. "Dawson is a peacemaker. I can't believe he's the target."

"Regardless, my mind's made up." Dan tapped his pocket for a Tums. "I'm hiring a PI."

The medical clinic hummed with patients all day Tuesday. Everybody seemed to get sick after a three-day weekend, and Gena was too swamped to think beyond the moment.

Her nurse and right-hand woman, Alabama, zipped around like a pond skimmer keeping everything in order, including Gena.

"Baby in exam room two. Temp 104 since last night. Mrs. Brannon in three thinks her gallbladder's acting up again, and in room four is a new patient." She glanced at the file in her hand. "Clare Hammond. She's new in town, a trim carpenter working for the Buchanons. Drilled a nail in her hand."

"A female carpenter. That's interesting."

"A fortunate woman to work with all those pretty Buchanon men—even if she shoots herself with a nail gun."

Gena scanned the chart in her hands. "One of those men is practically married."

"And one has his eye on you."

Gena had no time to think about Quinn. None.

More briskly than she intended, she asked, "Is the nail still in Miss Hammond's hand?"

Alabama blinked, clearly curious at the abrupt cutoff when Gena had filled her ear with Quinn news in recent days, but she didn't ask. "Nail is out. She only needs a tetanus."

"Get the injection. I'll have a look."

"The injection is set up and ready and so am I."

"Always ahead of me. You're amazing."

"Lunch is on your desk. You should eat."

"Later. Too busy."

"You say that too often." Alabama stuck a hand on her hip. "I am halting every patient except true emergencies until you at least drink the juice. No argument."

A small woman, when she squared her shoulders and got that firecracker expression in her chocolate eyes, Alabama Watts was a force.

"Drill sergeant." But Gena rushed into her office, swigged the juice and hurried to see the sick baby.

By two o'clock, the calls and walk-ins competed with regularly scheduled appointments for Gena's time. The receptionist began rescheduling those who could wait, something Gena disliked doing. As it was, she'd be here long after five. She'd need to call Derrick and let him know when she found a spare minute.

When her cell phone rang, she ignored it. Five minutes later, her office manager, Jason, met her outside exam room three.

In an undertone, he said, "The school called. Apparently, there was a problem. Derrick's run away."

A shot of adrenaline surged through Gena's veins. Not now. Not when she was this busy. But something serious must have happened. He'd been doing well.

"See which of my patients Dr. Ramos can fit in or send them to the ER. Reschedule those you can." Pivoting, she headed to her office.

"What are you going to do?"

"Find my nephew." She was already out of her lab coat, and in three minutes she exited the parking lot and drove up and down the streets around the school and past the football field.

Where would he go? Home? To Quinn's cabin?

Please not Houston. He'd spoken by phone to one of his so-called friends when they were in the city yesterday but he hadn't gone out.

Still, the lure was there.

What if he'd gone to the highway to hitchhike? What if even now he was riding south with some maniacal trucker?

"Stop it, Gena. You're scaring yourself." Calm and cool in emergency situations, she rarely panicked. Only Derrick could set her nerves on fire.

With the rhythm of her pulse battering against her collarbone and perspiration erupting on her lip, panic wasn't far away.

Pulling to the side of the street, she put the vehicle in Park and gripped the steering wheel with both hands.

"Breathe. Just breathe." Hadn't she said those words to her patients hundreds of times?

Inhaling deeply, she exhaled slowly. "Rinse and repeat."

After three long, deep breaths, she felt more under control, but dealing with this would be easier if she weren't so alone.

Now she understood why God intended kids to have a mom and a dad. Strength in numbers. When one hit a wall, the other could take over.

She needed someone who cared about Derrick, who cared about her. She needed Quinn.

She opened her cell phone and scrolled to Quinn's contact information. Her shaky finger hovered above the screen for long seconds while she battled whether to call him or not.

She pressed Call and then quickly pressed End.

Quinn would be at work for another hour or two. She couldn't bother him on the job.

"Jesus, help me find my boy," she prayed.

Hoping he'd run home, she decided to try there before searching the highways and interstates. She aimed the car toward the river bottom and soon crawled along the dirt and gravel roads. At the two-mile section, she spotted a lanky form plodding along the side of the road.

Breathing a sigh of relief, she pulled alongside him. Head low, he kept walking.

She rolled the window down. "Derrick. Get in."

He glanced her way, face stormy and perspiring. Glowering, he jerked the door open and slithered inside.

"What happened?"

He slid deeper in the seat.

Lovely. They were back to the silences again.

They traveled the remaining mile without conversation, though Derrick's anger was loud enough to fill the car's interior.

Once they reached the farm, he slammed out of the vehicle and stalked inside the house.

Shoulders slumped, insides still shaky and tumbling, Gena followed, wondering if she was the right parent for this unhappy child.

He stood at the sink gulping water. She put a hand on his shoulder.

"Let's talk about whatever happened. Did you have a problem with the history teacher again?"

He shrugged her off. "No."

"What, then? Talk to me."

He glared at the empty glass. "Didn't you call the school?"

"Yes, but the principal didn't know, either."

"He's clueless." With a sneer, he reached for the faucet. "Like always."

She put her hand over his, stopping the show of defiance before he turned on the water to drown out conversation.

"Derrick, there is no need to be disrespectful. I'm trying to help here, so stop acting like a spoiled brat and tell me what's wrong."

"You want to help?" He slammed the glass onto the counter and whirled at her. "You really want to help?"

Keep calm. Don't overreact. "You know I do."

His chest rose and fell. His face reddened and distorted. "Then tell me who my father is."

Gena sucked in a breath. Oh, no, oh, no. Had someone noticed the similarities between Quinn and Derrick?

"Did someone at school say something about your father?"

"Like, why don't I have one? And if I don't, what that makes me."

"You don't have to listen to that kind of talk."

"No? How am I gonna stop them? Huh? How? By telling them his name? 'Cause I don't know. But you do."

"Derrick." Her heart beat out of her chest, but on the

surface, she was Nurse Gena, calm as frozen water. "We've talked about this before."

"Yeah, and you lied." His eyes narrowed into slits. "I'm not a dumb little kid anymore who believes everything you say. Mom would have told you. You were sisters."

Shaking, Gena forced out the lie. "No."

Derrick slammed his fists against the side of his head over and over again, screaming, "You're lying. You're lying."

She grabbed for his hands but sports and anger had strengthened him. He jerked away and slammed his fists against the countertop.

"I hate my life. I hate it. I hate everything!"

Shocked and scared to see him completely out of control, she used her sternest voice. "Stop it, Derrick. Stop it right now. This behavior is doing no one any good."

He slumped to the floor and, head on his upraised knees, began to sob. "It's not fair. It's not right. Everyone has a dad but me."

Gena's heart twisted in knots. She slid to the floor with him. "You know that's not true."

His breath shuddered. "But at least they know who he is. Please, Gena, I'll be the best kid in the world. Please tell me."

Heartsick, she said, "Don't ask me to."

His head came up. Tears streaked his skin, dusty from the walk. "But you know. Mom told you."

"She made me promise. She loved you. You were her life. But your father hurt her badly."

"When he found out about me."

She'd already said more than she'd intended. She had to stop before it was too late.

She put a hand on one of his knees. "Derrick—

He shoved her hand away and glared at her. "He didn't want me, did he? He wanted her to get rid of me."

"Derrick, stop. We can't talk about this."

"Am I like him? Is that it? Was he a bad person? A criminal? A gangster? Is that why I'm such a rotten kid? Because my father was a creep? That's it, isn't it? I'm bad because he was?"

"No! No! Don't think like that. Your father is a good man, but he had a promising football career and he was injur…"

Gena froze, stunned by the slip and praying her nephew wouldn't pick up on the clue.

"Football?" Derrick sat up straighter, his face suddenly pale. "My dad played football? Like Quinn?"

"Not like Quinn."

"But you said—"

"I said, not like Quinn."

He stared at her with Renae's eyes while her heart hammered and hot blood rushed like Niagara Falls through her brain.

Oh, what had she done? What had she done?

White as a sterile bandage, Derrick went still and quiet. The stove clock ticked several long seconds.

"Is Quinn my dad?"

Gena got up from the floor, avoiding his stare, unsure of her next move.

"Is he?"

"This subject is closed."

"Is he? Is that why you didn't like him at first? Why you didn't want me over at his cabin?"

Gena went to the refrigerator on shaky knees and pretended to look inside. The rush of air cooled her burning face.

"Want some lemonade?"

Derrick scrambled to his feet. "Tell me, Gena."

She took out the pitcher, stalling for time, praying for an answer that didn't come.

"If you don't tell me, I'll ask him."

"Don't do that. Never, ever talk to Quinn about this, do you hear me? Never."

"So it *is* him."

Gena didn't answer. She couldn't.

She simply opened the cabinet, took down a glass and poured it full of lemonade. Tart and sweet, like Quinn.

Instead of the expected outburst, Derrick scrubbed a hand over his face, walked out of the kitchen and went to his room.

Gena stared at the filled glass in her hand. She couldn't swallow if her life depended on it.

She set the glass on the table and followed. Derrick's door was locked.

Guilt stricken, Gena stood in the narrow hallway, contemplating what to do. Even though she'd avoided telling him, he'd figured out the truth.

"Derrick?"

"Leave me alone." The sound came muffled through the door. Was he crying? Brooding? Both?

She placed her palm against the worn wood. The caregiver in her desperately wanted inside that room to comfort and heal the hurt. But some wounds cut too deep to be a simple fix.

Derrick was right. He needed time alone to process. He needed time to calm down.

So did she.

The proverbial cat was out of the bag, and she wasn't sure what to do about it. Derrick was as volatile as raw nitroglycerin. She didn't know what he'd do with the information, but she had to tell Quinn before he did.

Forgive me, Renae.

She had no idea how Quinn would react. Anger? Resentment? Both were likely, and he might hate her for keeping his son away from him. Or he could reject Derrick as he'd done Renae and shatter the boy into a million unrestorable pieces.

Nothing good could come from this secret now revealed.

But she had to tell Quinn first. If she explained about Renae's dying request, maybe she could minimize the damage. Maybe he would understand.

More important, she had an eleven-year-old who needed her. No matter how inexperienced she might be at parenting, she had to find her way through this lonely jungle for Derrick's sake.

Quinn would have to wait.

Chapter Sixteen

Quinn tapped the computer screen and moved a wall six inches to the left. With another tap and drag, he created a short foyer leading to a side staircase.

The floor plan was shaping up into something special. He might keep this one for himself.

The thought surprised him for a nanosecond before he said, "Why not? I have the land. I can build a house if I want to."

He wondered if Gena would like it. He thought she would, especially his-and-her walk-in closets big enough to live in.

Or maybe he was getting way ahead of himself.

The black-and-white kitten rose on her hind legs, rubbed her cheek against his and meowed, a tiny scratchy sound as if her throat was perpetually sore.

He scratched between her eyes with one finger. "A sunroom for you? I'll take it under consideration."

Hadn't Gena mentioned wanting a sunroom for her medicinal herbs?

He'd never intended to keep one of the cats, but no one else seemed interested and she was growing on him. Little thing. Runt of the litter.

"You'd never make the football team."

But she made up in grit for what she lacked in size. Sweet and feisty, she pounced on every spider and cricket that dared slither beneath the door into her domain and battered a toy mouse all over the cabin.

Yeah, he'd bought her a toy. And he'd named her Bella. So sue him.

He made a few more changes in the floor plan, ran a few measurements and cost-assessment figures before moving on to designs for Buchanon Built.

Dad's PI hadn't arrived yet, but they'd had no new incidents of vandalism. Brady and Abby were talking wedding and wanted the brothers as groomsmen. Good times.

Yeah. Very good times.

Lifting the kitten to the floor, he went to check the casserole in the oven. The smell had his belly growling like a mad dog. Since he'd kicked the pills, food tasted better than he could remember.

He was doing all right in that department, and he was pleased with his progress. Nights could still be long, but with Gena on the other end of the phone, foregoing sleep was easy, and taking her advice, he'd learned new ways to deal with his pain, both physical and mental.

Gena. He should call her tonight and find out what was going on. He hadn't heard a word since the voice message on Sunday morning. And here he was designing a house around her.

Had he done something?

He barked a short laugh. When hadn't he done something?

The woman was incredible for liking him at all.

He thought she loved him, and instead of wanting to run, he was happy. He'd even mulled the benefits of domestication.

Allison teased him today about whistling at work.

Bella padded silently across the room to stretch herself

across the top of his foot the way her mother had the night she'd given birth. He leaned forward to scratch her ears.

Out of the blue, the front door slammed back against the wall and reverberated like a gunshot.

Quinn nearly dropped to the floor, hands over his head. Bella skittered like a cartoon cat across the smooth wooden floor and hid under the table.

Derrick stormed into the cabin, all fury and fire.

Quinn held up a hand. "Whoa, tiger, what's got you all fired up?"

Derrick clapped fisted hands on his hips and glared, more belligerent than Quinn had ever seen. "Why did you leave her?"

"What? I didn't leave anyone." Was he talking about Gena? Was something going on that he didn't know about? "Is Gena mad at me? She's the one that stood me up, not the other way around."

Derrick's voice rose. "Don't play stupid. You know what you did. You had no right. You're a sorry creep. A good for nothing—"

The kid was on fire about something, and apparently, he thought Quinn was to blame.

"Hey, buddy, come on. Let's sit over here and calm down. I've got a great casserole in the oven, courtesy of my mother's leftovers." Quinn reached for the boy's elbow.

Derrick jerked back with a stunning violence. "I don't want your stupid food. I don't want anything from you."

Okay, that was it. He was starting to get mad himself. Leaning his face close to the boy, Quinn clenched his teeth and said, "You want to tell me what's going on? Or is this some kind of guessing game? If it is, I don't like it. If you got something to say, spit it out. Otherwise, go home."

The stern words didn't begin to penetrate Derrick's rage. He was on some unknown mission and wouldn't wind down until he was empty. "Why did you leave her alone with a rotten kid like me?"

Quinn watched the boy's eyes. He was about to cry. This wasn't an ordinary Derrick fit. Whatever had upset him cut deep.

Brain reeling, Quinn searched for meaning between the hurt and the rage and came up as empty as a hole in the ground.

"You didn't want me, so you dumped her. I get that. I'm a rotten kid. But why her? She was the best mom—" Derrick's voice cracked and he turned his head to one side, shielding his face with a hand.

Silence, broken only by Derrick's harsh breathing, settled over the cabin.

"Renae?" Was the kid talking about Renae and him?

You didn't want me, so you dumped her.

The words replayed in his head. Twice.

Cold realization slithered like a snake down Quinn's back. He licked lips gone dry as Sheetrock.

In a deathly quiet voice he asked, "What are you talking about, Derrick?"

Was the kid saying what he thought he was saying?

"You know."

No. Couldn't be.

Quinn's insides started to shake.

"Know what? Are you saying I'm your—" He couldn't get the words out. Had Renae been pregnant?

Impossible. Well, not impossible but unlikely.

She'd said nothing. She hadn't called. She hadn't visited him in the hospital. She'd walked out during the worst events of his life.

Had she been carrying his child?

Derrick slowly turned to meet his gaze with tear-streaked face and red eyes.

"You're my father." He tried to smirk but his lips quivered. "Ain't that a crying shame?"

The air went out of Quinn in the same way the fire had gone out of Derrick. All he could do was stare at the tall, lanky, handsome boy with the big, broken heart and Renae's eyes.

He had a son?

All during dinner preparations in which she cooked Derrick's favorite spaghetti and meatballs, Gena prayed. She wasn't hungry, not with the turmoil eating at her guts, but a boy nearly twelve would eat nuts and bolts and about anything else no matter how upset he might be.

When the garlic bread scented the kitchen, she went down the hall to his room and tapped at the door. "Derrick, dinner is ready. Spaghetti and meatballs."

No sound came from inside.

"Derrick? Come on. Open the door."

When he still didn't respond, she tried the knob. The door opened with one turn.

"Derrick—" His bed, messy from where he'd flopped, was empty, and so were his desk and the rest of the room. One glance and she knew how he'd gotten out of the room without her knowledge. The window was open.

"Not again." Then her common sense and intellect kicked in together. This time, she knew.

"Oh, no." Not there. Not to Quinn's place. Not before she had a chance to break the news gently. To explain.

She grabbed her keys and ran to the SUV. She had to get there before Derrick did, before Quinn learned the truth in the worst possible manner from a furious boy lashing out in pain.

She pressed the accelerator as if she was on a disaster call. In her heart, she feared she was. A disaster of the soul that could destroy a young boy's life.

If Quinn shattered Derrick's heart, she'd never forgive him…or herself.

When she reached the cabin, Derrick's bike lay on the ground next to the porch as if he'd leaped off in a mad rush and let the bicycle fall.

The front door stood open. Derrick and Quinn faced off like two prizefighters. Neither spoke, but emotion pulsed like a giant elephant's heart around them.

Insides quivering, she stepped inside. Quinn's gaze cut toward her, held and accused. His face was drained of color.

Gena's stomach fell, tumbled like a rockslide down Everest.

Quinn swallowed. "Derrick is my son?"

Slowly, looking between him and Derrick and back again, she nodded. "I wanted to tell you, but Renae made me promise to keep quiet."

He stared at her, scowling in bewilderment.

"Quinn, you have to understand. She was dying."

"And her last request was that I never know I have a son?"

"Yes." She bit down on her bottom lip, shamed by the hurt reflected in his eyes and by her own culpability in putting it there.

He scrubbed both hands over his face. His fingers trembled. The kitten sneaked from beneath the table to wind her small body around his legs.

"Why?"

Really? He would ask such a thing? "You know why, Quinn. You broke it off after the accident."

"She said that?"

"Yes. She didn't know she was pregnant at that point, and after the accident, you wouldn't take her calls. You refused to see her at the hospital."

He shook his head. "That's crazy. After the accident, I

was in a Dallas hospital for a month. She didn't visit. She didn't call. I figured she'd dumped me because I wasn't Mr. Football anymore."

"She wouldn't have."

He chuffed. "Everyone else did." Suddenly, he groaned. "I can't believe this."

"Believe it, creep," Derrick spat and wheeled out of the house.

Gena followed the boy as far as the door and watched him stalk across the yard where they'd played football, head down, shoulders slumped as if he carried the weight of the world.

Lord, what a mess. I don't know what to do.

She turned back toward the man standing in the middle of the cabin bearing the same dejected stance as his son.

"Don't hurt him this way, Quinn. Hate me. Hate Renae. But not Derrick."

"Is that what you think? You think I'll kick him in the teeth because Renae, and now you, kicked me when I was down?"

"She didn't. You're the one who ignored her when she was pregnant and scared."

"I don't know what she told you, but it's a lie."

"No!" She didn't want to believe such a thing about her sister.

"*My* world had ended, Gena, not hers. I was sick, wounded, confused and angry. I had nothing left to offer, no arm, no lucrative contract waiting to be signed, nothing." His face twisted. "Like all my other so-called friends, like the magazines and photographers and fans, the girl who claimed to love me was nowhere around. If she had even hinted at being pregnant…" He spun to the side and slapped both hands against the wall.

It was all Gena could do to keep from smoothing a hand down his back.

He was to blame, wasn't he?

Or was he?

She let herself remember Renae as she'd been during her college days. Her popular sister had always needed and expected men to chase her. She'd basked in the attention. Had bragged about dating the most popular guys at college. If they forgot to call or weren't attentive enough, she dumped them before they could dump her.

Renae claimed Quinn had been different, but had he?

"She tried to call you."

"When?"

"I don't know for sure. I think right after the accident." He frowned. "I never got that call."

"She was sick all the time, throwing up and scared to tell Mom and Dad."

"You knew. You should have told me."

The accusation cut. "She came to my apartment and confided in me, but it wasn't my place to contact you. She'd telephoned the hospital. You didn't want to talk to her."

"I couldn't talk to anyone! I nearly died, Gena."

Gena ran a hand over her head, holding on to the top to keep it from blowing off. Everything made sense now, but the realization was a stunning, heartrending miscommunication. Quinn and Renae had needed each other and both were too young and scared, sick and insecure, to reach out.

"I can't believe you kept this to yourself. Not after—"

She reached toward him, afraid now. "I wish I hadn't, but I did and nothing can change that. I'm sorry, really, really sorry. No matter how upset you are with me, please don't turn your back on Derrick. He needs you more than ever."

"You think I don't know that?" He scoffed. "You must think so little of me. And I thought we were…"

Hope leaped. "Thought what?"

"Nothing. Never mind." He shook his head slowly from side to side as if his brain was full of sand. "He's really my son?"

"This is a shock for you."

He laughed without humor. "You think? You and Renae and your family kept me away from my son for eleven years. Yeah, I'm shocked. Stunned. Seriously messed up."

"If I'd known…"

"You did know."

If I'd known you weren't the man Renae thought you were. If I'd known I was going to love you. But Gena didn't say any of that. He wouldn't believe her. Not after she'd destroyed the trust between them. "Renae made me believe—"

"That I was the Big Bad Wolf."

"Yes. I was wrong. She was wrong."

"You've known me for months. We've been…close. Doesn't that count for anything?"

Close? She'd been falling in love, and she'd thought he felt the same.

"I'll go now and take Derrick home. Maybe after you've had time to collect your thoughts and put everything into perspective, we can talk again."

"Talk?" His voice was harsh. "About what?"

"Derrick. About what to do and what you…want." She sighed.

"He's my son. That's what I want."

She held up a hand, stop sign–style, very afraid of what he might say. Would he take Derrick from her?

"Take some time. Get perspective."

His head snapped back in a huff. "Right. Perspective."

She exited the house and yelled for Derrick to get in the car.

"My bike."

"Forget the bike. We'll get it later. Just get in the car."
For once, he didn't argue.
The ride home ached with silence.

Chapter Seventeen

Quinn ran the river, and when exhaustion didn't erase the turmoil in his gut, he got in his truck and drove. First he drove idly, brooding and trying to piece together the muddy, cloudy months after the accident. He came up empty.

He flipped on his blinker and found he'd driven on autopilot to Brady's house. His brother was washing his boat, a sixteen-foot black-and-silver hybrid.

"Going fishing?"

"Tubing with Abby and Lila on Saturday. Want to come? You can bring Gena and Derrick."

"No."

Brady tossed the massive wet sponge into a bucket of sudsy water. "What's up? You look down."

Up. Down. That said it all. "I need to talk to somebody with more brains than I have."

Brady laughed and clapped him on the back. "My man, you have come to the right place. Pull up a piece of my porch."

He did. His much bigger brother settled his back against a porch rail.

"Beautiful out here."

"Yep. But my excellent taste in building sites is not why you're here. What gives?"

"Gena."

"You're in love with her. We already know that."

He snorted. "Yeah. *She* doesn't know."

"She probably does, but tell her anyway. Women like the words."

His brother the expert now that he'd found Abby. "Not that easy."

"You don't think she feels the same?"

"I did."

"She does."

"This isn't exactly about Gena. It is, but it isn't."

Brady gave him an appraising once-over. "No wonder you needed someone with more brains. You've lost yours."

"The problem is Derrick."

"Behavior issues? He's coming into adolescence. He'll get better."

Quinn studied his hands, long and strong. Derrick's hands were similar. So was his physique and the way he ran and threw a ball.

Why hadn't he seen the resemblance before?

"He's my son."

Brady made a hissing sound, like a tire with a giant hole in it.

"I never even suspected. Renae didn't bother to tell me. In fact, she swore Gena to secrecy." He squeezed his up-raised knees. "I have a son, Brady. Had I known, I would have been there for him. For Renae."

"Are you still in love with Renae?"

"Don't be stupid."

"But you're mad at Gena for not telling you."

"I don't know." He scrubbed a hand over his mouth. "Maybe. I'm not sure what I feel. Betrayed maybe."

"What are you going to do?"

"I don't know the answer to that, either. I wish someone would tell me."

Brady stared with ocean-blue eyes toward the horizon, where the sun showed off in red-orange flames of sunset.

Dawg sauntered around from the back of the house and dropped a stick in front of Quinn. Idly, he picked up the graying piece of limb and gave it a long toss.

They both watched the big brindle animal gallop in flop-eared delight toward the object.

"You still got a pretty good arm."

"Better than anyone thought it would be." He'd worked hard to achieve this level of fitness, as much as he'd worked hard to be a star quarterback. Same work ethic. Different goals.

Funny how all his goals had changed, morphing to fit his life after the accident.

"How's the pain? You seem better there, too."

"Gena's helping me with pain control—or she was." Gena. She occupied every other thought.

"Want my advice?"

"That's why I'm here."

Brady made a derisive noise. "You've never taken it before."

"A man can change. I hope."

"You have. Your mood's better, and unless my observation is way off base, you're getting close to happy. The whole family sees the changes and we like them."

"Are you talking about me behind my back?"

"That's what family does." Brady flashed a crooked grin. "Here's the advice. Get in that monster truck of yours and drive straight to Gena's house. Tell her you love her and want to work things out."

"You make it sound easy."

"It is. Do it."

Was he ready to forgive and forget? Just like that? "She

knew Derrick was my son and chose not to tell me. I'm having trouble getting past that."

Dawg trotted back, dropped the stick at his master's feet and sat, smiling and expectant.

Brady rubbed the animal between the ears. "What would you do if I was on my deathbed and asked you to make a promise?"

"You know the answer. I'd do anything you wanted."

"Would you keep that promise even if doing so caused you grief?"

Quinn didn't have to think. Without a doubt he would. "I get your point."

"Gena was between the famous rock and hard spot. Give her some grace." Picking up the stick, Brady gave it a fling. "Now get off my porch and don't come back until you and Gena have made up."

Quinn scratched at the back of his neck and got to his feet. "I was pretty rough on her."

"So? Eat that crow, brother, and all the humble pie it takes to set things right. Love's a whole lot sweeter to cling to than your pride."

She absolutely was not going to cry another useless tear. Not even one.

Gena turned down the music volume on her computer and wiped her face for the tenth time since coming home. She hadn't wanted Derrick to hear her crying, so she'd cranked high the peppy Mandisa album and listened to "Overcomer" repeatedly.

Some overcomer she was.

They'd had a long talk, she and her nephew, in which she'd assured him God would work everything out for their good. Right now her faith was a little low on fuel. Piecing together Renae's story with Quinn's, she'd explained the situation surrounding Derrick's birth as well as she possibly could.

Both parents wanted him. He needed to believe that.

She rose from the desk, then went to the window, opened the blinds and gazed out into the backyard. Nana's lavender irises bloomed by the mailbox next to the road, and Derrick and the kitten were where they'd been for the past forty-five minutes. The black kitten repeatedly pounced, moving grass while Derrick fired a football through the center of an old tire he and Quinn had rigged for practicing aim. The boy was working off his emotions, though nothing short of a miracle would fix the hurt a pair of college students had done to each other and to him.

In the kitchen, she poured two lemonades and carried the glasses out onto the back porch. Derrick glanced in her direction. She hoisted a glass. Without a word, the boy walked to the porch and flopped down beside her. He smelled sweaty and hot.

Gena handed him the lemonade. "Five in a row through the hole."

"I'm improving. Quinn says by next fall—" He caught himself and stopped, lifting the cold glass to his lips, though he didn't drink. For weeks, every other sentence had been about Quinn.

Now uncertainty hung in the air thicker than morning mist over the Red River Valley. What would Quinn do with the news that he was a father? Like his son, he'd been angry and hurt, and rightfully so.

His last words haunted her. *He's my son. That's what I want.* Would he do that? Would he, in anger and revenge, drag her into a custody battle?

The thought scared her to pieces. She was only the aunt. Quinn was the father. She didn't know much about law but was very much afraid Quinn had a case for custody.

Derrick gulped the lemonade and backhanded his mouth. "You really liked him, didn't you?"

She massaged a hand over the boy's slumped back. "Yes. I think you and I both did."

"Yeah." He sighed. "If not for me, he wouldn't be mad at you, and everything would still be okay."

"This isn't your fault."

His boyish face, kissed with a promise of the manly beauty shared by his father, swiveled in her direction. "Feels like it is."

While she searched for reassurances, dust appeared on the gravel road leading to the farm. In seconds, Quinn's truck came into sight.

Derrick hopped to his feet. "I'm out of here."

The screen door slapped shut as Quinn strode toward her across the lawn. Dusk crawled behind, a sheer gray curtain closing in on the day.

Gena remained frozen to the porch step, two half-empty lemonade glasses condensing at her side. As the man approached, she examined him as she would a patient. The pinch of pain around his eyes. The determined set of his jaw. The swing of arms, though one side did not quite match the other.

All the heartache and loss that arm had caused had come to roost on an innocent eleven-year-old boy.

Quinn glanced toward the elevated tire swing, pausing to pick up the football Derrick had left behind.

He came to stand in front of her, tall and intimidating the way he must have been on the football field. "We need to talk."

"Yes."

"I've been thinking about Derrick and arrangements."

This was moving too fast.

Gena stood up, putting them on more equal footing,

though Quinn towered over her. "We have to do what's best for Derrick."

"I agree."

A breath eased from her. "Good. He's the important one here. Not me or you or wounded egos."

"He's my son."

Her pulse spiked. "I have custody. He's my nephew. Renae wanted me to raise him."

"She also wanted me out of his life, and that's not acceptable. His mother is not here to make the decisions anymore. But his father is."

She flinched and crossed her arms against the fear snaking over her skin. "I'll agree to liberal visitation rights. You can be a part of his life. He needs that."

He stacked his hands on his hips and wagged his head back and forth. "Not good enough."

"Then what—?" She was afraid to know.

"There's only one acceptable arrangement. I want to be Derrick's father all the time. Full custody and nothing less."

As if he'd sucker punched her, Gena bent forward, hands pressed to her belly. The thing she had feared from the moment Quinn dragged Derrick to her door with a gun in his hands was about to happen. Quinn would try to take her nephew away.

Not acceptable. No way. Buchanons had power, but they were not God.

Fists clenched, she spun on him. "I'll fight you."

Quinn caught her hands and held them, surprisingly tender as he pried her fingers open and rubbed his palms over hers. "I suspect you will. Most couples fight now and then."

Gena stopped struggling. "What?"

"Derrick needs a mother and a father. I was hoping.

Maybe. You and me. We could do this parenting thing together."

She relaxed a little. "You mean joint custody?"

"Sort of, but not exactly. What I have in mind is more… personal." Inch by inch, like a fisherman reeling in a bass, he drew her closer.

She tilted her head back, looking up at him as a seed of hope took root. "I'm not sure I follow."

"You and me. Maybe I'm jumping the gun, maybe it's too early, but I think we have something…special. If you don't feel the same, tell me now before I make an idiot of myself."

"I do. Or I think I do. How *do* you feel?"

He laughed a little and shook his head. "As if I can't get through the day if you're not somewhere in it. Like a man who has finally found an answer to a question he hadn't thought to ask. You. You're my answer."

"And you're mine." He always had been.

"For so long, I've let myself be half a man because of the injury. I couldn't see beyond the crippled arm, but then you came along, gave me a swift kick or two that opened my eyes and made me want better."

"Did I really do that for you?"

"And more. I'll never be all I once was—"

She touched his jaw, covered with evening stubble. "You're more. You're better. A better man, a better person. God's man."

With a slight twist of his head, he placed his lips against her fingers. "I don't want to rush you. We can take our time with this thing if that's what you want, but I have to say the words or my big brother will be on my case forever. And I won't get a bit of sleep tonight."

She knew what he wanted to say. As she watched him struggle past the walls he'd created around his emotions, she waited, loving him even more for the effort.

Finally, he blew out a long breath and said, "I love you, Gena."

She tilted her head, heart singing, smiling more each moment. "So that's what you meant about full custody?"

"Right. You, me and Derrick. Mom, Dad and son."

"Are you proposing?"

"Are you accepting?"

She almost laughed, but the topic was too serious. "Can I think about it?"

His face fell, but he didn't back off.

"If you think I'll change my mind when emotions are not running as high, you're wrong. I'm in love with you, Gena. L-O-V-E. Examine it under your microscope, grow it on a petri dish, roll it around in that big brain of yours or whatever you need to do. My feelings are not going to change."

"What about Derrick? If I say no— If you and I aren't together, what happens to him?"

She saw the struggle behind his eyes. Pride and paternity and a host of other emotions she couldn't identify. She had to know for sure if he loved her for her or as a solution to a custody issue.

"I don't have a hard-and-fast answer, Gena, but I promise you this. No matter what happens between you and me, I want to be included in Derrick's life, but I would never take him away from you."

Quinn Buchanon, grown-up and mature, was ten times better than Mr. Football, the self-absorbed object of her teenage crush. His love, both for her and for Derrick, was bigger than his pride, bigger than her fear.

She slid her arms around his waist and smiled up at him.

"I've thought about it long enough." She tiptoed up until her lips were mere millimeters from his. "I love you. We'll work out the rest as we go."

He breathed a major sigh. "You scared me for a minute."

"I had to be sure."

"You called an audible. I like it," he murmured right before he kissed her.

While she sank into the man, thrilling to the full realization of what had transpired, the screen door banged against the side of the house.

"I got one question." Derrick's voice penetrated the sweet cocoon of love.

Reluctantly, Gena pulled away from the man and turned toward the boy.

Keeping her close, arms loose at her back, Quinn said, "Shoot."

"So." The boy perched a fist on one hip. "Is my name really Derrick Buchanon?"

Quinn and Gena exchanged looks, communicating without words.

Quinn dipped his chin. "It can be."

Derrick gave a nonchalant jerk of one shoulder and sniffed. "I'll think about it."

Both adults laughed. In spite of his cool, Derrick laughed, too.

"Come here, twerp." Quinn opened his arms.

"Is this like a group hug or something cheesy like that?"

"Family hug. Real cheesy," Quinn said. "Now get in here where you belong."

Derrick came, awkward and eager and, if she wasn't mistaken, thrilled out of his mind as Quinn welcomed his son into their circle of love.

Epilogue

June in Texas, even North Texas, is hot. With this in mind, Quinn's brother and his bride had opted for a small, indoor wedding with only family and a few friends in attendance. Abby insisted on simplicity she could afford without using Brady's money.

She was funny about paying her own way. As Brady had informed him on more than one occasion, he didn't care if they married at the courthouse in work clothes. He wanted Abby as his wife, his forever friend and love. The wedding was simply a means to an end—and a new beginning.

Quinn understood now in a way he never had before.

Gena, at his side, where he planned for her to stay, pointed toward the bride's table. "They're cutting the cake."

Cameras flashed, followed by applause as the couple crossed arms and fed each other their first bite as husband and wife. His attention on his brother's laughing face, Quinn didn't notice the young woman sidling up next to them.

"Nurse Gena."

Gena smiled a welcome. "Miss Hammond, so nice to see you again."

"It's Clare, please." To Quinn, the woman said, "Gena

patched me up after I shot a nail into my hand." She presented the palm, more rough and calloused than his. "Good as new."

He recognized her, but barely. On the job, Clare Hammond wore a T-shirt and jeans with work boots, her hair slicked up on top of her head. Today she looked much different in a lacy dress and heels with straight auburn hair lying against her shoulders and shiny earrings dangling from her ears.

"You work for Johnny French, right? Carpentry crew."

She nodded and the earrings danced. "Subcontracting on the houses your brothers don't have time for."

"My dad and brothers are particular about subs. You must be good."

The hint of a smile lifted her mouth. "I like to think so."

"She's making Dawson and me look like sluggards." Sawyer appeared out of the small crowd to join them. "Hi, Clare. You look gorgeous."

"So do you."

Sawyer's movie-star teeth flashed. He offered an elbow. "Let me escort you to the cake and punch, my beauteous colleague."

"Where you will tell me all about the custom router design you created for the McBride house?"

"Trade secret, but I might be convinced to share if you ply me with enough punch."

Quinn snorted. "You gotta watch out for that nonalcoholic ginger ale punch Mom makes."

Sawyer nodded sagely. "Powerful."

Clare hooked her arm in his and they wove through the people with Quinn watching.

"Did you detect sparks between those two?" Gena asked.

"Sawyer sparks anytime a pretty single woman comes around."

"Too true."

"Enough about my brother. Where's our boy?"

Since discovering he had a son, Quinn worked to make up for lost time and to heal the wound he'd unwittingly caused. Fondness quickly grew to a deeper, stronger attachment and in time he believed they'd be true father and son, if they weren't already.

He didn't blame Renae now that he understood the chain of events. She'd been as young and scared as he had been.

"Derrick's with Ryan. Don't worry. He's on his best behavior."

"In a suit and tie? I hope so."

His son still had rough edges, but the porcupine quills showed less often. Quinn wished he could say the same for Gena's parents. His reception in Houston had been chilly but he wouldn't give up. Gena and Derrick were worth any amount of groveling required on his part.

Gena leaned into him and whispered, "Doesn't Abby look beautiful?"

Quinn nodded his agreement.

He wasn't an expert on wedding dresses other than he couldn't wait to get Gena into one, but Brady's bride was a stunner. The former waitress who considered herself oversize and gawky was neither of those things. Today she glowed with confidence as she stood next to a bridegroom who couldn't take his eyes off her for more than a second at a time.

Tall and slender, though nowhere near as tall as Brady, the brunette bride wore a long, fitted gown in the palest mint green. Lila as flower girl wore the same color in a fluffy little-girl princess dress. Metal leg braces had peeked out as she'd moved down the aisle, tossing summer rose petals and stopping to say hello to everyone she knew.

At the moment, the little charmer scooted her walker

around the tulle-decorated fellowship hall with Charity's daughter blowing bubbles from a tiny vial and giggling.

Lila was a heart wrecker. Every Buchanon adored the special-needs child with the enormous personality.

"I wouldn't mind having a little girl someday." In fact, the idea kind of nestled under his rib cage, warm and sweet.

Gena pretended to straighten his tie. He liked when she fussed over him. "Maybe two little girls?"

"And a couple more boys. Coach says we need more boys like Derrick for the team." Fatherly pride biased his opinion, but Derrick had major potential.

Gena laughed. "Girls can play ball, too. I beat *you*, didn't I?"

"Once. But you cheated." He pecked a kiss on her nose and turned serious. "I'm not sure I want to encourage Derrick toward sports beyond high school anyway."

"Why not?"

"Me. Without the accident, I'd be in the NFL."

"Making millions."

"Exactly the problem. What good is it if a man gains the whole world and loses his soul? In retrospect, I was traveling the road to self-destruction. I couldn't see it before. Fame, money, adulation and being treated like a superhuman who could do no wrong as long as I threw touchdown passes. Dangerous combo."

"Fame and money alone are not evil, Quinn."

"No, but I was arrogant and self-serving without the character to handle everything that comes with success."

"Are you saying God took the opportunity away to save you from yourself?"

"I don't know. If He did, I'm grateful." He laughed shortly. "Hard to believe I'd ever say that about this crippled arm."

She tapped her shoulder. "Put that crippled arm around here, big guy."

He obliged.

"See?" Smelling like summer flowers, she turned into his arms and tilted her face. "Not so crippled after all. You can still hold me tight."

He smiled down at her. "Are you sure you don't want to get married today?"

She chuckled, but her green eyes glowed like emeralds. "And steal Abby's thunder? Uh-uh. But soon."

"A diabolical plot to make us men get all dressed up again."

"Of course." She patted his chest. "You look so pretty in a tux."

He caught her hand and held it against his heart. "For you, I'd wear sackcloth and ashes." He made a silly face. "Whatever that is. So when are you going to marry me?"

Her smiled curved, full and beautiful and tempting, but before he could break his no-PDA rules, he spotted Derrick swaggering toward them through the crowd, grin wide. An entourage of preadolescents trailed him.

"Hey, Dad."

Time froze. Quinn drew in a breath, holding the moment in his lungs and against his heart, unleashing a butterfly flutter of inexplicable love for a mouthy, tender boy with a heart of gold. His son.

After months and years of not wanting to feel, he wanted to experience all of this, to remember forever the first time his son called him "Dad" while the woman he adored looked on in smiling, loving approval.

He glanced at Derrick, then at Gena, and saw his life with a fresh clarity. He'd soared to the heights and fallen to the depths. He'd succeeded, and he'd wallowed in failure. But everything he'd experienced, both good and bad, was merely a stepping stone in the journey to today. To this boy and this woman. To where he belonged.

The best moments of his life began now, and, by God's grace, he was finally man enough to receive them.

* * * * *

THE BUCHANONS *miniseries continues next year, and don't miss* New York Times *bestselling author Linda Goodnight's next book from HQN Books,* THE INNKEEPER'S SISTER, *in March 2017!*

Dear Reader,

Some years ago, a minister of my acquaintance required post-op pain medication, a perfectly legitimate use of strong narcotics. Unfortunately, after a time, this man became addicted to the pills. When he could no longer get the pills, he began to use illegal drugs to ease his pain and feed the addiction that had taken hold of him. He lost his ministry, his family and eventually his life. No one who knew him could believe this had happened to such a good, God-fearing man. But it did.

With Quinn Buchanon's story I wanted to address this real issue that is sometimes considered taboo in Christian circles. The truth, of course, is that Christians are humans subject to the same fragilities as everyone else. Our victory is that we have a means of escape, a Savior if we reach out to Him and ask for help.

I hope you've enjoyed *Lone Star Dad*, and if you or someone you love struggles with a drug problem, please reach out. Hope in Jesus is waiting.

Linda Goodnight

www.lindagoodnight.com

COMING NEXT MONTH FROM
Love Inspired®

Available October 18, 2016

THE RANGER'S TEXAS PROPOSAL
Lone Star Cowboy League: Boys Ranch
by Jessica Keller
When Texas Ranger Heath Grayson finds pregnant widow Josie Markham working her ranch alone, he insists on helping. Josie's vowed never to fall for a lawman again, but she soon realizes he could be the final piece to her growing family.

AMISH CHRISTMAS BLESSINGS
by Marta Perry and Jo Ann Brown
In these two brand-new novellas, Christmas reunites one Amish beauty with a past love, while another will be led headfirst into her future by a handsome Amish farmer.

THE COWBOY'S CHRISTMAS BABY
Big Sky Cowboys • by Carolyne Aarsen
Former rodeo star Dean Moore is eager to find a new path after an accident cut his career short. Reuniting with former crush and single mom Erin McCauley to fix up her home in time for the holidays could be his second chance with the one who got away.

THE PASTOR'S CHRISTMAS COURTSHIP
Hearts of Hunter Ridge • by Glynna Kaye
Retreating to her grandparents' mountain cabin for Christmas, city girl Jodi Thorpe is looking to rebuild after a tragic loss. She never expects to be roped into a charity project—or that the pastor running the program is the former bad-boy crush she's never forgotten.

A MOM FOR CHRISTMAS
Home to Dover • by Lorraine Beatty
As she heals from an injury, ballerina Bethany Montgomery agrees to put on her hometown's Christmas extravaganza before heading back to her career. But when she discovers old love—and single dad—Noah Carlisle, is also back in town, can she make room for a new dream: becoming a wife and mom?

HIS HOLIDAY MATCHMAKER
Texas Sweethearts • by Kat Brookes
All little Katie Cooper wants for Christmas is a mommy. But Nathan Cooper isn't prepared for his daughter's matchmaking—or to find himself under the mistletoe with interior designer Alyssa McCall as they work on the town's new recreation center.

LOOK FOR THESE AND OTHER LOVE INSPIRED BOOKS WHEREVER BOOKS ARE SOLD, INCLUDING MOST BOOKSTORES, SUPERMARKETS, DISCOUNT STORES AND DRUGSTORES.

LICNM1016

REQUEST YOUR FREE BOOKS!

2 FREE INSPIRATIONAL NOVELS
PLUS 2
FREE
MYSTERY GIFTS

Love Inspired®

YES! Please send me 2 FREE Love Inspired® novels and my 2 FREE mystery gifts (gifts are worth about $10). After receiving them, if I don't wish to receive any more books, I can return the shipping statement marked "cancel." If I don't cancel, I will receive 6 brand-new novels every month and be billed just $4.99 per book in the U.S. or $5.49 per book in Canada. That's a saving of at least 17% off the cover price. It's quite a bargain! Shipping and handling is just 50¢ per book in the U.S. and 75¢ per book in Canada.* I understand that accepting the 2 free books and gifts places me under no obligation to buy anything. I can always return a shipment and cancel at any time. Even if I never buy another book, the two free books and gifts are mine to keep forever.

105/305 IDN GH5P

Name _____ (PLEASE PRINT)

Address _____ Apt. #

City _____ State/Prov. _____ Zip/Postal Code

Signature (if under 18, a parent or guardian must sign)

Mail to the **Reader Service:**
IN U.S.A.: P.O. Box 1867, Buffalo, NY 14240-1867
IN CANADA: P.O. Box 609, Fort Erie, Ontario L2A 5X3

**Are you a subscriber to Love Inspired® books
and want to receive the larger-print edition?
Call 1-800-873-8635 or visit www.ReaderService.com.**

* Terms and prices subject to change without notice. Prices do not include applicable taxes. Sales tax applicable in N.Y. Canadian residents will be charged applicable taxes. Offer not valid in Quebec. This offer is limited to one order per household. Not valid for current subscribers to Love Inspired books. All orders subject to credit approval. Credit or debit balances in a customer's account(s) may be offset by any other outstanding balance owed by or to the customer. Please allow 4 to 6 weeks for delivery. Offer available while quantities last.

Your Privacy—The Reader Service is committed to protecting your privacy. Our Privacy Policy is available online at www.ReaderService.com or upon request from the Reader Service.

We make a portion of our mailing list available to reputable third parties that offer products we believe may interest you. If you prefer that we not exchange your name with third parties, or if you wish to clarify or modify your communication preferences, please visit us at www.ReaderService.com/consumerschoice or write to us at Reader Service Preference Service, P.O. Box 9062, Buffalo, NY 14240-9062. Include your complete name and address.

LI15

SPECIAL EXCERPT FROM

Love Inspired

*What happens when a Texas Ranger determined to stay
single meets a pregnant widow who unwittingly works
her way into his heart?*

*Read on for a sneak preview of the second book in the
LONE STAR COWBOY LEAGUE: BOYS RANCH
miniseries, THE RANGER'S TEXAS PROPOSAL
by* **Jessica Keller**.

"What can I do for you, Officer?" Josie Markham's tone
said she didn't really want to do anything for him. Ever.

He raised his eyebrows.

"White hat. Boots. White starched shirt. And that
belt's the type they only issue to Texas Rangers." She
gestured toward his holster. "I hope you weren't trying
to be undercover."

"Good eye." He extended his hand. She narrowed
her gaze but shook it. "Heath Grayson. I'm a friend of
Flint's."

In the space of a heartbeat, her hesitant expression
vanished and was replaced by wide-eyed concern. "Did
something else happen at the boys ranch?" She shifted
from around the wheelbarrow. "What are we waiting for?
If something's wrong, let's go."

Once she moved away from the wheelbarrow, he
saw her stomach. Pregnant. Very pregnant. Flint had
mentioned Josie was widowed, but he'd left out the little
detail that she was with child. So a recent widow.

LIEXP1016

Had she been in the barn alone…doing chores?

"Let me help you with your chores," Heath said.

Josie's jaw dropped. "What about the boys ranch?"

"The ranch is fine."

"Why didn't you say so? You about gave me a heart attack." She laid her hand on her chest and took a few deep breaths. Then her eyes skirted back up to capture his. "If the ranch is fine, why exactly are you here then?"

She fanned her face and dragged in huge amounts of oxygen through her mouth as if she was having a hard time getting it into her lungs.

Now he'd done it. Gone and gotten a pregnant woman all worked up. Did he need to find her a chair? A drink of water? Rush her to the hospital? What a terrible feeling, being out of control. It was disconcerting.

"Are you all right, ma'am? What do you need?"

"I'm fine. Just fine." She laughed. "You should see your face, though." She pointed up at him and covered her mouth, hiding her wide grin. Her warm brown eyes shone with mischief. "Now you look like you're the one having a heart attack. Relax there, Officer. It was only a figure of speech." Her laugh was a high sound, full of joy. Josie laughed with her whole self, without holding anything back.

Heath wanted to hear it again.

Don't miss
THE RANGER'S TEXAS PROPOSAL
by Jessica Keller, available November 2016 wherever
Love Inspired® books and ebooks are sold.

www.LoveInspired.com

LIEXP1016